HAMMETT PRIZE FINALIST

"[An] understated and compassionate historical novel."
WINNIPEG FREE PRESS

"Showcases Palka's great attention to detail,
which enhances an already beautiful and deeply
moving story of hope, love, and triumph."
BOOKLIST (STARRED REVIEW)

"Palka's book contains wisdom and elegance."
TORONTO STAR

THE ORPHAN GIRL

BOOKS BY KURT PALKA

Rosegarden

The Chaperon

Equinox

Scorpio Moon

Clara (originally published in hardcover as *Patient Number 7*)

· *The Piano Maker*

The Hour of the Fox

THE ORPHAN GIRL

A NOVEL

KURT PALKA

McClelland & Stewart

McClelland & Stewart and colophon are registered trademarks of
Penguin Random House Canada Limited.

Published simultaneously in the United States of America.

Library and Archives Canada Cataloguing in Publication data is available upon request.

ISBN: 978-0-7710-7253-6
ebook ISBN: 978-0-7710-7254-3

Book design by Talia Abramson
Cover art: (woman) © Marie Carr / Arcangel;
(waterfront) George W Johnson / Moment / Getty Images
Typeset in Bembo by M&S, Toronto

Printed in Canada

McClelland & Stewart,
a division of Penguin Random House Canada Limited,
a Penguin Random House Company
www.penguinrandomhouse.ca

1 2 3 4 5   26 25 24 23 22

Penguin
Random House
McCLELLAND & STEWART

For Heather

ENGLAND
1944/45

One

IN THE NIGHT SHE STOOD at the kitchen window at the back of Claire's house and in the dark saw her own reflection; the gauze taped over the injury on her cheek and a glimmer in her eyes when she moved her head. Far away she could see the moon reflected in a silver track on the Talbot River. A difficult night. She should have stayed in bed, but it wouldn't let her. She knew what it was and she shouldn't have let it in, but tonight once again she couldn't keep it out.

"And you?" David had said to her the last time she saw him. "Can I ask how you're doing with it. With Trevor?"

He never called him her dad or her father, always just by his name.

"I'm doing all right."

"Got to the bottom of it yet?"

"There's a bottom?"

"Very deep down. You'd probably drown getting to it. But I think you found a way to swim to shore, and the water has gotten shallow and now you can walk. Keep on walking, Kate. I think you're almost on dry land. He's gone, you know."

"I know that. Most of the time. In my head."

But not tonight; a tidal night dragging her back into the deep. The silver track on the river was the trundle path and she was the girl of that day and she was walking the path with her father. As they often did. He had just said something to her about another war shaping up in Europe, and that he was being sent once more to Germany on a diplomatic mission to gauge the situation first-hand and then to report back, when she heard footsteps behind them. A moment later two men in long coats and hats passed them on either side, as if encircling them, and when the men were a dozen paces ahead, they both turned and one of them took his hand from his coat pocket and raised a handgun and fired twice. And immediately the men hunched their shoulders and hurried away.

Her father had fallen down, and in shock and disbelief she knelt by his side. She could see it so clearly again, the blood pulsing from his chest while she tried to keep it in with her flat hand, but there was blood flowing also from his mouth and nose and she tried to stop it with her other hand. Then she realized that he couldn't breathe and she turned him on his side and turned his face downward for the blood to flow and clear his airways, but it didn't help. She cried for help as loud as she could, screamed and wept for it in horror and disbelief.

The two men were gone from sight and she was alone with her dad dying. He tried to say something and she put her ear to his mouth but heard only his blood. She stood up and screamed again for help, waved her arms and knelt down and raised his head and held it in her lap, and this would forever be her last image of him, his head in her lap as he lay dying.

Eventually a man and a woman came along the path and saw them. The woman talked to her and held her, trying to calm her while the man went to fetch the police.

The policeman asked questions and wrote down her answers. An ambulance came and two men took her dad away. There was blood on the hard soil of the path and in her shocked state she thought they should take that as well, because they'd have to get it back into him. She called to them and pointed at the blood, and they looked at her strangely.

The murder of the diplomat Trevor Henderson was in all the papers, but the police never found out anything. Perhaps they never even tried very hard, or they knew what it was and weren't allowed to say.

For months afterward she believed that she could have saved him if she'd kept her hands on his chest and perhaps a knee as well, and pressed hard. Or bandages. She could have made bandages from her coat sleeves or something. She wished she'd done that, any of that; wished it lying awake nights, feeling guilty and useless. She cried often and only narrowly passed her examination for the Higher School Certificate; she, a former good student. Then her mother found Dr. Elliott at Riverdale Hospital.

The doctor was wonderful. He sat with her and he listened, nodded and asked questions. He took his time and thought about what she was saying. She was enrolled at St. Anne's College by then, and a few weeks into their sessions Dr. Elliott suggested she might be interested in the evening course for ambulance and paramedic training.

It was the summer of 1939, and the situation in Europe was deteriorating rapidly. Hitler was amassing weaponry and armies, and despite the Munich Agreement armed conflict seemed ever more likely. The United Kingdom was preparing for it, and the ambulance corps accepted her with open arms. During the course she came to see that without plasma and fluid replacement there had in fact been nothing she could have done to save her father. And most likely not even then. Two bullets through and through. Four wounds and two bullet paths tearing organs and arteries. So much blood loss, internal and external. Learning that helped her.

In session after session the instructors taught the students about medical emergencies and first aid, how to find people in the rubble of a bomb site and how to get them to a hospital fast. Along the way she also earned her driver's licence and learned how to drive a seven-ton Bedford ambulance truck.

When St. Anne's College was closed because of the war she decided to make paramedics her full-time career. She took every last course they were offering and she worked hard to be not only a good first-aider, but also to be the best and quickest ambulance driver she could be. Speed saved lives. From the garage men she learned about truck engines and transmissions, learned how to double-clutch when downshifting to maintain momentum and speed, and she learned the London streets by heart; the turns and the shortcuts, and where rubble blocked streets. Especially during the horrors of the Blitz in 1940 and '41.

By then, David Cooper, a university professor and long-time friend of her parents, had come from Canada to help out. He lived with them, and because he was kind and intelligent and never pretended to be able to replace her dad, they got along well.

She turned from the window and left the kitchen. *David, yes. Think of David instead,* she told herself. *Even though he's gone for now, he'll be back. He will, you'll see.*

In her bare feet she walked through the hall to the entrance door, opened it, and listened down the dark, silent stairs to the garden gate and the street. Held her breath and listened.

"Claire," she said. "*Claire?*" But of course there was no one. Claire worked long hours, and this week she was on night shift. During one of their getting-to-know-you talks in the kitchen Claire had told her that she'd lost two children of her own, still as babies, and now could have no more. The tragedies had changed her life absolutely and perhaps forever, she'd said. But work helped. She was a medical doctor and specialist in the treatment of severe traumatic injuries, and she worked at three different hospitals. There was a husband, who was in the war, and when Claire had mentioned him, there had been a sudden change of mood, a darkness and an editing that left gaps in the information. Kate had noticed that, but she hadn't followed up.

Back in her room, crawling into bed, she glanced at the lighted dial of the clock, and as always in a tidal night the time was between two and three. Always.

She lay back slowly. Claire had said that the bandage around her cracked ribs could come off soon. Good. Even though sometimes, such as now, her chest still hurt and so did her back. She shifted a bit and bent her right knee. There. Better now. A slow breath, careful and as deep as the bandage would allow. She closed her eyes. Darkness. *Be calm,* she told herself. *Calm inside. Go to sleep.*

Two

ONLY FIVE MONTHS EARLIER it had still all been very different. On a Sunday in October 1944 David had telephoned her at the paramedic station to make a date with her, and at the end of her shift they'd met outside a building a few corners from King Street, the high street in their town. She'd come there on her bicycle, in her uniform; David, as usual, wore a jacket and tie.

He unlocked the street door and led the way along a dim corridor. He stopped at another door and quickly, with a small motion that she almost missed, he knocked softly three times in a distinctive rhythm: *one . . . two, three.* He unlocked the door, then pushed it open and stood back. She entered the room and he followed and waved a hand like a proud host.

"My writing room, Kate."

She looked around: a wood floor, cracked plaster walls with laths showing in places, a window with faded tab curtains half open, a desk, a chair, and a filing cabinet. On one wall there was a large corkboard with rows of index cards, and on the desk stood a black Underwood typewriter and a lamp. The single window looked out onto the service lane.

"What are those?" she asked, looking at the corkboard.

"Chapter cards for what I'm writing. I'm excited about it, but it's kind of secret. All of this is. The room and my work here. You are only the third person to know about it. You, your mother, and Tony, the landlord."

"It's interesting. How long have you had the room?"

"Not that long. A few months."

He took a letter opener from a desk drawer and walked to a corner. "There's something I want you to see. Come, take a look."

He knelt down, slipped the letter opener between two floorboards, pried up the short one and set it aside. He lifted out two more, and then in the space under the floor she could see a bundle of papers tied with string.

"My manuscript," he said. "The working title is *Dostoyevsky and Friends*. They weren't really friends, of course; some weren't even contemporaries, or barely so, but they had a lot in common. It's not finished, but I wanted you to know where it is."

"In this hidey-hole. Why so mysterious, David? Why not just keep it in the filing cabinet?"

"There's nothing in the filing cabinet. Or in the desk drawers. I like this better. It's safer. And the manuscript is not ready to be shown to anyone yet."

He fitted the boards back, ran his hand over them, and stood up. "I always make sure the spaces between them are exactly the same. That way I can tell if someone's been looking at it."

"Someone like who?"

"You never know. Academia is full of nasty people." He put the letter opener back into the desk drawer.

Later they sat at one of the four metal tables on the pavement in front of the tea room. They were the only patrons there. David was pouring tea from a Brown Betty into his cup while she sipped Horlicks from a mug, and loved it.

She could tell he was in a thoughtful mood, probably about his manuscript. When he'd first arrived he taught English and philosophy at St. Anne's, and when the college was closed he carried on tutoring motivated students privately in their homes, helping them stay sharp, as he called it, for when the emergency was over. He'd studied Russian and German so he could draw on the literature of those cultures as well, and because English professors speaking Russian and German weren't easy to find, he sometimes also went on certain assignments for the government that he said he couldn't talk about. He said it had to do with building bridges abroad for when the war was over.

"In that way he's a lot like your father," her mother once said to her. "Not quite that bad, because David deals with academics and writers that he admires."

"What writers?"

"All kinds. Whereas your father had to deal with politicians, which was probably how he made enemies. Bringing back classified information to various government departments, until one day he probably knew too much, or knew the wrong thing. I'm not saying he and David were the same, just very similar. But what can you expect? Both coming from the same nest."

"By *nest* you mean Oxford?"

"Yes. In the days after the Great War they took aside some of the brightest at our universities and swore them into secret lifelong obligations. Told them it was an honour. Those that were reluctant were shamed into it."

But during the meeting at the tea room there was no talk of any of that. Instead David told her that, while his current writing project served the relentless academic pressure to publish, it also allowed him to dig into the lives of some of the brilliant outsiders and seekers he admired. Men and women, all with a rebellious streak, like Nietzsche, Kierkegaard, and Dostoyevsky, and Lady Anne Conway, Mary Wollstonecraft, and others.

He said his manuscript was examining how they'd done it, where it had come from and what it had been that kept them on track, each of them doggedly following their own compass and ignoring all else.

"Fascinating people," he said. "Solitary, determined, brilliant. Bringing philosophy down to earth and putting handles on it. Making it actually useful, like a tool for living."

He poured more tea, and then he said the strangest thing, something she would never forget . . .

Across the little table and their chipped pottery, and with sunlight dappling them kindly through a maple tree in autumn colours, he said that if he were to die or disappear for some reason, he wanted her to burn every last piece of paper in that secret room.

"In a corner behind the building there's an old steel drum with air holes in the side for draft. You can see it from the window. Kate, are you hearing this? It may sound strange but it's important. Start with a few crumpled pages, and pour coal oil over them and drop in a match. Then feed the fire with just one or two pages at a time until they're all gone. Make sure you separate the pages and crumple them. They won't burn completely if there's no air between them."

She sat back and shook her head. "What?"

"You heard me. If I should die or disappear, I want you to burn it all. Make sure every last piece of paper in that room is gone."

"What's all this dying and disappearing stuff? Are you serious?"

"Yes, I am very serious. You never know, and academia is a jealous beast. I want no paper of mine to be seen by anybody if I didn't submit it myself. There are always far too many eagerlings waiting to trash one's work and reputation."

"So that's why you're hiding it in that cubbyhole?"

"That's one reason, yes."

"What's the other?"

"Mainly that."

"In case you die or disappear you want me to *burn* everything. The manuscript and the chapter cards too? Did I hear that right? Burn it all? Do you have copies somewhere?"

"No, I don't, and yes, you did hear me right. I want you to burn it all. It's important."

"And why would you be dying or disappearing? What's going on, David?"

"Nothing's going on."

She sipped from her mug and put it down, took her time arranging it precisely between two rust spots on the table. She looked up at him. "David, it's me you're talking to. Kate. What's going on?"

"All right, all right . . . What's going on is that I may have to go abroad again, soon. I wanted to tell you about the manuscript and the room because I trust you. Now that it's done I can rest easy. And there is something else . . ." He stopped.

"What?"

He thought for a moment and frowned down onto his hands. Then he said, "Never mind. It'll keep."

"No, what?"

"It'll keep, Kate. For when I'm back." He looked different to her suddenly. She, a practised face-reader, saw something new in his eyes, like a fear moving across. Her dad had taught

her about face-reading a long time ago: if one remained absolutely calm inside, he'd said, and observed a person closely, one
could tell not only what they were feeling, but often also what
they were thinking. And one could tell not in the higher centre
of one's brain, but in the lower. Sense it, with one's reptile brain.
And so she sat very still now and studied David's face, his eyes.

He reached and touched her hand on the table. "Don't do
that. It makes me nervous."

"So what is it? Does Mum know that I'm supposed to burn
your work in case you don't come back? Even just to put that
into words . . ."

"I know. And I'm asking only you. *You*. It's like writing a
last will and depositing it with a trusted friend. Think of it as
a simple precaution and there's nothing to worry about. And
listen: your mother will know, but never tell anyone else about
the manuscript. Or the room. No one. Keep it a secret." He
paused, then he said, "Please promise me that you'll do that.
I need to know and feel confident about it."

And so she did. She took a deep breath and let it out, and
then she said, "I don't like it, but I hear you. And all right . . .
yes, I'll do it."

"Promise?"

"Yes, I promise."

"Good." He smiled at her. "Thank you. Case closed."

———

For a moment they sat in silence, a gap in time. Hardly any traffic. A few bicycles and the clip-clop of a horse and carriage, the man hunched on the bench, the woman and two children huddling in the back among bits of furniture. The iron rims grinding on the road. A war-worn look to everything, and suddenly the drone of military aircraft coming closer . . . very loud now . . . several of them in formation . . . then receding.

As if shaken loose by the noise, a golden maple leaf came tumbling down. Turning slowly, slowly, settling on their table like a gift. She picked the leaf up and twirled it by its stem, looked at it closely, then put it into her uniform cap where it lay upside-down on the table.

David nodded at the black bruise on the back of her hand and said, "What happened there?"

"A little accident. The other day a site collapsed on two people who'd been sleeping rough there. We dug them out and they were all right, but then the end of a beam came down on me. Luckily there were no pegs or nails in it. It's not too bad anymore. We took an X-ray and there's nothing broken."

She flexed her hand to show him.

He said, "Good, good," and nodded, and it was then that he asked the question about how she was doing with Trevor, and in asking it created the word picture that would always stay with her: the image of her knowing she could never reach the bottom of what had happened to her dad, of this unknowable depth, without risking drowning. An act of acceptance on her part, and of coming up for air and swimming until she had sand under her feet, and then walking safely ashore.

It was true and it was perfect. It was original David, the way his mind worked, and it was an example of why she found him interesting and liked him so much.

Tony in his white apron opened the door, leaned out, and asked if David wanted more hot water in his teapot or she another Horlicks.

They told him that yes, they did. She cocked her head and said, "Is that . . . Leave the door open, Tony, please. I love that song."

And she sat back and listened as from the Victrola in the back of the tea room there came the voice of Vera Lynn singing about bluebirds over the white cliffs of Dover, a song that never failed to move her. She sat still with her eyes closed, and sang along inside her . . .

When the song was over and the door was closed again she said, "David, about your room and the manuscript . . . if it should ever come to it, I'll do what you're asking me to do, but let's not talk about it anymore. No more talk of dying or disappearing. In that song just now, did you hear and feel the air and sunlight around the words and the images? And hope?"

He looked at her and smiled. "Kate. Katie . . . of course I did. And I hear and feel it every morning when I smell the coffee. Even the fake stuff smells pretty good, and then I hear you and your mother puttering around the house, and I slip all that into my pocket as my talisman for the day."

He poured more tea. The added water had made it very pale.

"And why do you knock on your own door?" She tapped his rhythm on the table. *One . . . two, three.*

"Ah. You noticed. I don't do it all the time. Just sometimes. Call it superstition. Or out of respect perhaps."

"Respect for what?"

"For what the room is all about. To me. Which reminds me . . ."

He reached into his pocket and took something out. He opened his hand and there were two keys in it, tied together with a frayed little ribbon. He put them on the table.

"For you. And feel free to use the room, if you like. While I'm gone."

"So you *are* leaving again. It's a fact and you know it. Why don't you just say so?"

He made a face and said it was because he wasn't sure. But probably yes.

A farewell gift of sorts, she would always think: the keys and the request and the affirmation of his friendship and trust in her. The mention of her dad and swimming towards shore, and making peace with it. And the talisman in his pocket.

"All right, Kate?"

She nodded. She swallowed hard because she found this moment very difficult. She felt hot in her uniform, and the shoes were heavy and she knew she wouldn't be able to swim to shore in them, and she felt like crying.

He looked at her and he knew it, and he looked away to give her space.

After a while he said, "Kate, what I'm doing isn't anything like what Trevor had to do. It's not dangerous. I'm simply going to conferences to talk to people there."

"But there's a war on. And talk about what?"

He looked at her and shook his head. Then he said, "All right, Kate?"

And she nodded.

"Good. Thank you. The building where the room is, is owned by Tony here. He's a good man who's become something like a friend over the years, and he can be trusted. The rent's paid until next summer. It's not much anyway. It was an empty storeroom that he didn't need."

He looked at his watch again. He'd done that several times already. This time he saw her noticing.

He said, "Patrick is in town. I told him where we'd be and he said he might join us."

"Patrick?"

"Pat Bailey. From our old Oxford group. The three of us: Trevor, Patrick, and I. You met him a few times when Trevor was still alive."

A moment later he was looking past her, towards the street. She heard the distinctive sound of a taxi diesel engine, and his expression changed again; a sudden pallor this time, and tiny muscles in his face flickering, widening his eyes for an instant. He smiled but she could tell it wasn't really a smile at all.

"Speak of the devil," he said. And then with a sudden intensity and hardly moving his lips, he said, "*The keys, Katie. Quickly. Put them in your pocket.*"

She did, then she turned to look over her shoulder. The taxi was driving off and his friend was coming up to the table. He wore a Canadian military uniform.

"Pat," said David. He stood up. "I'm glad you found a taxi. There aren't many left now. You remember Kate?"

They all shook hands and Patrick swung in another chair and sat down. He took off his cap and put it on the table next to hers. Short blond hair, good features. A major, from the little crown on his epaulettes.

"Kate," he said. "It's been years. I was very sorry to hear about Trevor. Very sorry. Then I heard about you having become a paramedic. Good for you. Good work, that. Difficult and dangerous, I'm sure, but important."

There was kindness in his look, and for a moment something else. An indecision, she felt. A question followed by a quick calculation followed by a change of mind, and already it was gone. He smiled and nodded, and turned to David.

She watched them talk while she sipped the last of her drink, tipped the mug all the way to drain it completely. So good. And now maybe she should leave them to it. Bicycle home and wait for David to come home too.

She picked up the maple leaf and her cap, nodded at them and pushed back her chair. Patrick stood up, too, and for an awkward moment it seemed as though he might reach out and give her a hug, but then he just offered his hand. David looked on. Looked at her right tunic pocket where she'd put the keys, looked up at her face. So troubled, she thought. So different, suddenly. Why? As if hoping to be rescued from something.

What? What is it? she wanted to ask him, bend to his ear and whisper it to him. For clarity. But she didn't. No, she did not. And every single day thereafter she would wish she had.

Three

THAT NIGHT David did in fact leave. Or was taken away. He came home so late that she was already asleep and never even said goodbye.

But at some point, pitch-black outside her window and the small sounds downstairs. Low voices and whispers and footsteps, and then the front door opening and closing. By the time she was at the window all she could see was David walking away between two men in long coats and hats in the dim light from the lamp above the front door. The man on his left was holding his upper arm as in an arrest, a forced removal.

She opened the window with fluttering hands, an annoying double window with locking bolts that always jammed. Already they were climbing into a car, David and the man to his left in the back, the other man in front. By the time the outside window finally swung open the car was moving off; it moved without a sound, and no light ever came on, not even the narrow little wartime lights in front and back.

She left the room and stood on the landing in her bare feet and called down the stairway.

"Mum? Are you there?"

There was no answer and so she went down the stairs. Her mother was in the living room, in her old blue housecoat and slippers. Ready for bed with her makeup removed and her hair down and tied back. She was about to turn out the light, but when she saw Kate she took her hand away from the wall switch.

"We woke you. Sorry, dear."

"No, you didn't, but you should have. What's going on? Where are they taking him?"

"He's going on one of his trips. Toronto and Reykjavik, I heard them say."

"And who were those two men? Long coats and hats is a nightmare image for me ever since—"

"Shh!" Her mother raised her hand. "Don't say it. Let's not imagine things. Maybe they really were simply government people with his instructions for the trip. It happened so quickly. He said to say goodbye to you and to give you a hug for him. He left you a note." Her mother indicated a piece of paper on the table.

The note said, *Had to go, Katie. It's just the usual and I'll be back soon. Love, David.*

She held the piece of paper with both hands and looked up. "One man was grabbing his arm, as if he didn't want to go but they were marching him off. In the middle of the night, and you're not worried?"

"Well, of course I'm worried. Who wouldn't be?"

"Was Patrick here too, his friend from Oxford?"

"Pat Bailey? No. Why do you ask that?"

"Because when I left the tea room they were sitting together and David looked miserable. Mum, what do you know that you aren't telling me?"

"Nothing, dear. Nothing. Let it go. Let me give you that hug for him, and then go back to bed. It's late. He'll be back soon."

But he was not; he was gone a long time, much longer than usual. November came and went, and then one morning just before Christmas the postman brought a letter with the government seal on the envelope.

Her mother ripped it open.

In just a few short lines the letter said that there had been an unfortunate development. David Cooper had gone missing, but the authorities would keep up all efforts to find him. They had Mary Henderson as his next-of-kin contact, and they would keep her informed.

Kate rang the telephone number at the bottom of the letter, but no one answered. She rang several more times that day, and at one time a woman picked up and said she would pass on Kate's request for more information.

Next day her mother became ill. Once when she stood up from a chair she fainted. Kate caught her and helped her to bed. She took her pulse and then searched the list in the medicine cabinet for the telephone number of her mother's doctor. She found the number, but when she tried to ring it the operator told her that the number was no longer in service. Kate hung up and walked into the bedroom.

"Any other doctor, Mum?"

Her mother was lying back against her pillow with her eyes closed. "What, dear?"

"Another doctor. Dr. Ward is probably retired. What about the one before him? Dr. Ambrose?"

"No, not him. I never liked him."

"So what about that woman doctor, Dr. Giroux?"

"That was a long time ago, and then she specialized into more important things. But I did like her. We were on a first-name basis. She's from France originally, and then from Canada. Grew up in a piano factory. Claire is her name."

"Want me to try her? She's nice. I see her sometimes at different hospitals."

"I wouldn't want her to feel obligated just because I knew her in the past. Drop what she's doing, for this?"

"Mum, let me try her. You don't look well, and when I took your pulse it was fast and irregular."

Kate made a few calls and eventually found the doctor at Riverdale Hospital. Two hours later Dr. Giroux rang the bell.

———

The examination did not take long, and when the doctor came out of the bedroom Kate sat waiting on the chair on the landing. She stood up.

"This must have been an awful shock for your mother," Dr. Giroux said. "For you too, of course. How are you doing?"

"I think I'm fine. Worried of course, about David and now Mum."

"Of course you are. Mary's blood pressure has always been low but suddenly it's alarmingly high. One sixty-one over eighty and, you are right, her heart rate is much too fast and irregular. One thirty just now. As you'll know stress and emotional upset can be a trigger of serious problems, even of strokes and heart attacks once we get a bit older. She needs bedrest and something to calm her. Is there someone who could stay with you for a week or two? Lend a hand? Are you on call today?"

"Yes, later. I'm on nights this week. But I could ask my aunt Catrina, Mum's cousin. She stayed with us before."

"Good. I wrote out a prescription. Come with me, and I'll bring you right back so Mary won't be alone too long."

On the way to the chemist's Kate sat in the passenger seat of the doctor's motorcar. A black Wolseley with the official medical sticker on the windshield that would entitle her to get petrol when it was so strictly rationed. Good leather seats, a rosewood dash, and chrome around the instruments. There was hardly any traffic, and the doctor drove fast and well. A nice-looking woman, beautiful even. In her late thirties, or early forties maybe. Good skin and shiny dark hair held up with combs of shell. Good clothes, too: a wool coat over a charcoal skirt and a matching jacket and a lacy blue blouse.

"The medicine we're picking up," said the doctor. "Give your mother twenty drops in half a glass of water, three times a day. And keep her warm. Tell your aunt too."

"I'll do that."

"Let's see how her sleep is. I'll come by again tomorrow. I'll also sign a few extra food vouchers for you. Get your aunt to make a meat stew or a roast. Red meat and vegetables. A good thick gravy with the drippings and some Bisto in it. Food that'll stick to her ribs."

When they were back and the car was stopped in front of her house, Kate said, "Dr. Giroux, what's in Toronto and Reykjavik?"

"What do you mean, what's there?"

"Well, are they dangerous places?"

"Oh. I don't know, Kate, but I wouldn't think so. The one's a big city in Canada, and the other is the capital of Iceland. Iceland is neutral in this war. And Canada is a dominion and an ally. Halifax is an important North Atlantic harbour. Why do you ask?"

———

Upstairs Kate put twenty drops into half a glass of water and gave it to her mother. She sat in the chair at her bedside.

"Mum, are you sure you don't know anything more about Toronto and Reykjavik? Why he went there?"

Her mother stopped sipping for a moment. She made a face with the taste of the potion. Then she said, "He went there on a lecture tour, like always. That's what I understood. Ring that number and ask them."

"I did. Several times already. All they do is take messages but I never hear back. At one point someone answered saying 'Culture and Recreation.' So who knows."

"Culture and Recreation don't sound like big priorities when there's a war on."

"And you don't think that Patrick Bailey had anything to do with it?"

Her mother took more sips. She looked wearily at Kate. "I don't really know very much about Patrick. Even though I've known him for as long as I've known David or Trevor. I met them all at Oxford, when I was working in the dean's office. But you know all that. They got their PhDs at the same convocation. Boys in borrowed gowns, one crazier than the other. But interesting crazy, I'll admit. Wild and very bright. Be careful with boys, Kate. With men. Trusting them. Have I said that before?"

"Maybe a hundred times."

"Well. Can't say it too often. You've seen it with your Tom. Hopes all the way up, and where is Tom now?"

"He was never really *my* Tom, and I never had my hopes all the way up. Not after a while. Anyway, he met someone else. I told you at the time. A blonde. I saw them together once. Pretty, and because she's a civil servant she can be much more useful to him. And you know something?"

"What?"

"It's actually a relief."

Her mother chuckled. "Good. You're learning. It all seems wonderful and harmless, and it can be the one but it's never the other. The consequences down the road will change a woman's life forever. They just take over, completely."

"I know that, Mum."

"No, you don't. We think we do, but we don't. Nobody knows it until after the fact. That's one of nature's little backhand tricks. But I'll tell you something else . . ."

Her mother finished the potion and held out the empty glass for Kate to take. She gathered her hair to one side over her shoulder, leaned back into her pillow, and closed her eyes. Her hair was beautiful and still mostly black, except for a few fine strands of grey, nearly silver in the window light.

Kate waited, then she said, "What, Mum? What else were you going to tell me?"

Her mother did not open her eyes.

"Mum?" said Kate.

And very quietly and evenly her mother said, "The other day at the tea room, David was supposed to tell you about us planning to get married when he comes back. It was why he wanted to meet you on a special date. To tell you. But then he didn't, because he was being shy about it."

"Mum! You're getting married?" She leaned close and squeezed her mother's hand. "That's wonderful! But why would he be shy about telling me?"

"Because he knows how you feel, or felt, about your dad."

"He did ask me how I was doing with that. He said something very beautiful. About not drowning but coming up for air and then walking toward dry land."

"What else did he talk about? I know you told me some of it, but tell me again. I like hearing it. Poor David."

"He showed me the room where he's writing. He was proud of it, and he asked me to look after it while he's gone."

"And he asked you to burn all his papers and his manuscript if he doesn't come back."

"He did. And I promised."

"So what are you going to do now?" asked her mother.

"I'll wait, of course. He'll be back. I can feel it."

Her mother said nothing for a while. Then she said, "Good, Kate. I'm glad." She opened her eyes and struggled a bit to sit up. Kate rose and reached out to help, but her mother waved her away. "No, never mind. I'm tired. Listen to us, rattling on. No more talk now. No more questions, all right? And about Patrick and Oxford—about the four of us—look in the album in my small black suitcase. I think it's in my closet or maybe in the cellar, on the shelf against the wall. Take a good look at the photographs. It's all in there. Everything. And when David is back, we can have a good sit-down talk, the three of us, like we should have done a long time ago."

Four

FOR A WHILE then she was on the early morning shift, with her weekends free. She liked that shift because it gave her more time to spend on the horse farm, her second job. Mrs. Fitzhenry paid her sixpence an hour, and her job was grooming and exercising horses.

A mild winter so far and hardly any snow. Some days before or after the horse farm she'd bring a mug of Horlicks from down the street to the secret room, plug in the electric heater Tony had lent her, and sit at David's desk with her feet up. When the light was on she'd close the curtains, but when the light was off she liked them open, and she'd take her time sipping the warm drink and looking out the window into the back lane. Metal dustbins out there, his fire drum with holes in the side, and a street lamp at the end of the lane. Pigeons fluttering.

She liked this room. A monk's cell to concentrate the mind. Mostly just the typewriter and an empty page calling to you.

She studied his chapter cards and brought out the manuscript from its hiding place; fingered it and read into it. Good work in this. Written from within the characters, foot-marked and referenced. Or at least what looked like references at the ends of chapters, written not in English with the typewriter, but written by hand in Cyrillic, like a private code. But then this was only a draft.

One day she tried something new. She rolled a sheet of paper into his Underwood and typed him a note, like talking to him.

```
Dear David,

Mum is feeling stronger now. Aunt Catrina is staying
with us, and it's nice to have her there. She is a good
cook and Dr. Giroux's extra food coupons are coming
in handy. I like the doctor a lot. When she comes to
check on Mum, she often stays a bit longer and we
sit and talk. She asks me how I'm doing, and about
my work. She calls Mum Mary and me Kate, and Mum
calls her Claire, and so the other day she asked
me to call her Claire, too. At least when we are
in private.

    Yesterday Mum went to the lawyer with me, and
when I asked why, she just said, "In case something
happens." She signed some papers and I had to sign
```

them too. One was about Willowbank, your horse farm
in Canada.

   I'm considering opening an account for my savings,
but everything is so uncertain these days that
I think I'll just keep my money in my purse. So I can
buy a dress for your wedding. Why didn't you tell me?
When it's such good news!

She paused to read what she'd written. She liked this, talking
to him and to herself at the same time. Getting thoughts out,
clearing her mind. She looked at her watch, then used the shift
lock and typed the final line in caps:

I HAVE TO RUN, BUT WHERE ARE YOU? MUM AND I
TALK ABOUT YOU OFTEN. SO FOR HEAVEN'S SAKE,
ENOUGH NOW. COME HOME!

She cranked it out again, signed it *Missing you, Kate*, and
tacked it to his corkboard, next to the last chapter card and the
maple leaf.

Five

THE HORSES in the paddocks knew her bicycle bell and they stood looking her way, all eighteen of them, with their heads up and ears pointed. It was always something to look forward to. When she arrived, Mrs. Fitzhenry and one of the farmhands were busy in the barn. Kate called out to them and waved. She leaned the bicycle against the barn wall and Princess came trotting up to the gate.

Kate took off her gloves and put out her hand, and the horse sniffed it and tested it with her lips strong and nimble as fingers. "Look at you," Kate said to her. "You've been rolling in something."

She ran her hand down the horse's neck and shoulder and brushed off grasses and dry dirt. Then she reached into her pocket for the little apple she'd brought. Princess took it and started crunching.

The yearlings and the pregnant mare were due for a weighing, and so she unlatched the gate to the north paddock where the yearlings were and walked up to them. Tara and Sparkle, the girls, Redfire and Coffee the boys.

She weighed the yearlings first, walked them onto the scale and stepped off and watched the arrow settle down. While they were in a growth spurt, yearlings were expected to gain around one pound a day, and these four were doing just that. She wrote down the numbers in the log and walked the horses back outside. Their paddock adjoined that of their mothers, who raised their heads and whinnied at them across the white rail fence.

The pregnant mare's weight was on track as well. Her name was Amber, and she was in her third trimester, over the course of which the foal inside her would grow by sixty per cent of its birth size and weight.

Back in the shed Kate checked the list again and then scooped the right amounts of feed containing oats and protein and oil pressed from flaxseed into the containers numbered by paddock. She carried the containers outside and dumped the feed into the buckets hanging on the paddock fences. The horses stood waiting.

So as not to ride Princess too soon after feeding her, Kate lent a hand in the barn, moving hay from the hay floor to the stalls. Afterward she led Princess to the tack room, put her into cross ties, and brushed her. All along she talked to her, just calming words and sounds. She took off the rope halter and put on the good bridle and bit and then lifted blanket and saddle from the saddle tree and swung them onto the horse's back. A few pulls on the girth, and after a while another pull to gain an extra hole for the buckle prong. She led the horse outside.

On the mounting block she held the reins in her left hand on the withers, stepped into the near stirrup, and swung the right leg over and found the other iron. The horse never moved.

Mrs. Fitzhenry in her coverall and mucking-out boots stood in the wide-open barn door, holding a bucket. A strict woman. Determined, too. Her husband had died years ago and she'd carried on with the farm, working all hours with the help of only two regular farmhands.

"Good girl," Kate said to the horse. "Let's go, and be nice. She's watching."

And at the lightest touch of rein and legs they were off, down the Seven Oaks path, and up Shepherd's Hill and down again, into the valley. A fine dusting of snow in places, but the ground still good under the horse's unshod feet.

Riding along, Princess and she were in full agreement, the horse's powerful muscles moving, obeying the slightest nudge, the animal now nodding its head, walking the bridle path among the trees, birch and oak, all bare this time of year. Once they were clear of the trees she moved Princess up into a trot and then into a canter. Across Ravens Field, when they were nicely warmed up, she pushed her into a gallop with the breeze in her face and hair, the horse's mane tossing and its strong heart pumping in the massive barrel under her.

Six

FOR MANY MONTHS NOW no enemy aircraft had even attempted to penetrate the nation's airspace anymore, but the night of February 17, 1945, one did.

At 0234 hours a single Focke-Wulf 190B, a "suicidal last-minute raider," as the newspapers later called it, lit up the radar screen at the Dymchurch coastal defence station southeast of London. An alarm was triggered and forwarded in waves and sounded in towns below, and within minutes a patrolling RAF Hawker Hurricane sighted the German plane. It was still far from London, and the Hurricane moved up behind it and began firing its twenty-millimetre cannons. The Focke-Wulf was weighed down by two high-explosive bombs in a rack under its belly, and to get away from the Hurricane it veered off sharply and lightened its load.

The first bomb landed in the soft soil of an allotment garden, and failed. The second bomb fell through the roof of a house and exploded there with a massive shock wave.

———

By then Aunt Catrina had been staying with Kate and her mother for three weeks already, cooking and fussing, and her mother was feeling better. Because Aunt Catrina was using Kate's bedroom, Kate slept on the pull-out couch in a room next to the eat-in kitchen in the basement. She didn't mind; the basement was clean and dry and fully useable. It was below ground on the street side but had a level walkout at the rear. During the Blitz they'd all practically lived down there and slept there, night after night. It had been on the BBC so often: *If you're caught at home and you don't have an Anderson or Morrison shelter, take cover under tables or under beds, as low as possible in the house.*

That night, when Kate woke to the familiar sounds of the air raid alarm and of airplanes above, she quickly crawled under the table next to the couch and made herself as small as possible on the linoleum floor.

But that night was different. She knew it somehow, felt it, and then behind the sound of the air raid alarm she could actually hear the terror whistles in the bomb's stabilizers as it came screaming down. Louder and louder. Then the house exploded. Some elemental force slammed into her face and body, and her hair caught fire. She was pinned down under bricks and wood and plaster and could not move any part of herself. She swallowed blood and could hardly breathe with the grit in the air. Darkness and a hollow silence were all she could see and hear.

KURT PALKA

As minutes passed and stretched into time uncounted, she began to be able to make out a shape. Eventually she understood that that shape was her right hand, her index finger in front of her face, and over time and more time alone in the dark she learned to move that finger, and she made it her friend.

Of day or night she had no idea. Once in a while she vomited blood, and at times she passed out and came to again. Something was wrong with her cheek, because she could stick her tongue right through a large opening in it.

For support and company in the dark she talked to her finger, at first in silence, but eventually she also found her voice, weak and broken, and like dust far away.

Later she would remember trying to call out to her mother and aunt. How had they fared, and were they even still alive? And she'd remember thinking *So this is what it's like*, and she'd remember shouting for help and then fainting from lack of breath, and from then on only whispering. *Under here! Please! HELP! Under here!*

The warden's incident report said that two female bodies were removed from the site. With all the changes in the population it was not known how many persons had lived in the house, but the house was now a site of massive destruction with densely packed layers of rubble and collapsed floors, and in the warden's opinion it was unlikely that anyone could still be alive under all this.

But two days later, an eight-year-old boy walking home from a friend's house searched the bomb site for something interesting, some little trophy to take home, and he crawled deeper and deeper into it. He found a good hammer and a bicycle bell, and so, small and eager as he was, he kept searching. At one point he heard something and he stopped to listen . . . a muffled cry, then silence. He carried on, then stopped again . . . another cry.

Seconds later he was back up in daylight. He stashed his treasures where he could collect them later, then he ran to alert the neighbours.

And so finally they did come for her, neighbours and wardens. This time they brought a dog, and they spent hours working their way down through the rubble, careful, careful, with crowbars and pickaxes and an improvised pulley system.

And they found her; the dog did. She was unconscious again, but there was a heartbeat.

They rushed her to Riverdale Hospital and left her on the stretcher while orderlies bolted together another cot and put on a straw mattress. They transferred her onto that and it was while lying there that she regained consciousness.

She could not move and could hardly breathe with chest pains. She knew where she was because she'd often delivered patients to Riverdale, and she recognized the vaulted ceiling.

She closed her eyes, and when she opened them a woman in a white coat stood looking down at her.

"*Orderly!*" called the woman. "Orderly! Over here! Warm water, soap, and a sponge. And eye rinse and gauze and bandaging."

"I'm Dr. Giroux," the woman said to her. "What is your name?"

She told her, and the doctor looked at her closely and recognized her only now. "Kate!" she said. "Oh, my dear Kate. What happened? Come, let me help you."

A basin of water was set down and Dr. Giroux asked her to turn sideways over it, if she could. The orderly helped to steady her and the doctor rinsed her eyes and face again and again, and dabbed her dry. She put drops into Kate's eyes and told her to blink several times; more drops and more blinking, and still more drops.

"Breathe for me," said the doctor. She watched Kate's expression, then touched her chest lightly. Kate winced.

"Hmm . . . hurts a lot, does it? We'll take an X-ray to see what's going on. Now I want to inspect your cheek more closely . . . Hmm. I'll have to work on that a bit. But I'll rub in an anaesthetic and it won't be too bad." She turned to the orderly and said, "Please go and fetch Monica. And tell her to bring scalpel and scissors. And some anaesthetic paste and swabs, and surgical thread and a curved needle. And water for the patient to drink."

Kate lay with her eyes closed.

"No moving now," said the doctor. "Turn your head sideways with the bad cheek up, and press into the pillow and hold very still."

A nurse in scrubs brought a tray with instruments and set it down. Dr. Giroux leaned forward on the chair, and soon Kate could see them in silhouette from the corner of her eye against the dim ceiling of the hall, nurse and doctor, the doctor murmuring instructions and cleaning the wound and then pressing at her cheek and aligning the wound lips, and more dabbing and then beginning to put in stitches, needle and sutures pulling in the flesh of her cheek. It hurt, all of it, but she felt in good hands.

"Almost finished," said the doctor. "Just a few more pokes. We want to get it all good and level for a smooth heal. Keep holding still. I think you've got some cracked or maybe even broken ribs. Your hair is burnt in places, but the scalp looks all right and the hair will grow in. And there are several cuts and bruises but nothing too terrible."

Later that day the doctor came back with Kate's supervisor at Paramedics and with a woman from the town hall office, and it was then that Kate learned that her mother and aunt were dead and that the house was gone, and that a little boy from the neighbourhood had saved her life. The woman from town hall told them that the German plane had been shot down and had crashed and burned in a field south of Woolwich. The pilot had not ejected and had perished in the crash.

"What else?" said the woman. "Oh, yes. Your mother and aunt are in graves 945 and 946 in the east section of the cemetery. Now that we know the names, we'll put markers there."

Kate's supervisor had listened to all that, and now she said, "Terrible. Just terrible. I'm so sorry for everything that's happened to you, Kate. I'll tell them at the office, and in terms of money I know they'll continue to pay you at least half your salary for a while longer. Then we'll see."

After that Dr. Giroux came to see her every day. She examined her and sat with her and changed the bandage on her cheek.

"No sign of infection," she said. "And the X-rays are fine, Kate. You have some cracked ribs, but they'll knit and in a few weeks we can take the tight bandages off. You're getting better, and they'll be wanting you out of here any day now. If you've noticed, patients come and go all the time. You need to think about what's next. Do you have any family or friends that could help you out?"

The doctor looked at her for a long moment and saw the unspoken answer. She turned away, put the stethoscope into her bag and snapped it shut. She said, "You could stay with me for a while. Maybe until David is back and things get sorted. See how that works."

"Stay with you?"

"Yes, Kate. I knew your mother and I liked her. And I know a bit of your story now, and I like you too. I live in a three-bedroom house with two bathrooms in the Pineview part of town. There's a garden with a gazebo and a stone angel, all surrounded by trees. I have a husband and he'll be home whenever this war is over. I'm sure we'll all get along fine."

That was how it began; how they entered each other's lives, and how their lives would become entwined in friendship and in a love and closeness that neither of them had ever experienced. So simple. Both would always remember this moment: Claire speaking those words from kindness and from private longings of her own, and Kate hearing that the doctor was offering her a home until David was back. A place of shelter to find her way back to herself and to heal in much more than just her body. Claire in her white coat sitting in that rickety chair by her cot, looking at her with so much kindness that her eyes filled. She closed them.

"I'm so very sorry for all your loss," she heard Claire say. "Words cannot—there *are* no words for it."

A loudspeaker was calling, "Dr. Giroux! Dr. Giroux to the main entrance for an emergency! Dr. Giroux!"

And Kate heard the chair scrape as Claire stood up and pushed it back against the wall . . .

Seven

TWO DAYS BEFORE CLAIRE brought Kate home, she took heart and began to organize the room that had been meant to be the nursery for her own children. The first had been stillborn and no one had been able to tell her why. The second, also a little boy, had died as a three-week-old from a rhesus factor incompatibility, in her very arms, on a day with rain on the window. He simply stopped breathing and turned pale and still, and in that moment a weight had settled upon her heart that would perhaps never lift. The sound of rain on a window was always part of it.

William, she'd called him. Little William. She'd nursed him and held him in her arms, and tickled his cheek and bent to kiss his face and whispered *little sweetheart* to him.

Now she walked up the stairs and opened the bedroom door. An empty room except for the bentwood chair by the window where she sometimes sat, day or night but never when it rained. An east-facing window, for the promise of morning silver rising into the dark.

No other furniture in here anymore. Nothing; the crib and the change table already gone, picked up by a young woman some time ago. The woman had been seven months pregnant and she'd been shy and rosy, blooming with life and hope. She also took the sun-and-moon-and-stars mobile that Claire had hung from the ceiling over the crib and that no baby of hers had ever played with. And the bedding and all the baby clothes except for one little sleeper and a pacifier with a soft little rubber bear on it.

Five trips up and down for the husband, a strong young man. Nice, but a bit unsure about all this.

At four o'clock, Edward, the son of a patient of hers, came as promised and helped her with the bed. It was up in the attic, stored under dust sheets. They lowered the stairs and brought down the pieces and put them together and put the mattress on.

"There's a little night table up there too, Edward," she said. "And a couple of chairs. Oh, and my old student desk with the legs off. Can you help me with all that as well?"

Edward did. Afterward she gave him a shilling; he thanked her and slipped the coin into his pocket. They sat on the chairs in the room.

"Who is she, Dr. Giroux? The girl you're taking in. Can I ask?"

"Yes, of course you can. Her name is Kate Henderson. She's your age, I think. Her father was a diplomat and some years ago he was murdered. Now she lost her mother and her aunt as well, and her house and everything in it. That late bomb fell on it, the one we all heard in the night."

"Terrible. What bad luck. Was she hurt?"

"Yes, she was. Don't be shocked when you meet her. Or at least don't let her see it. I knew her mother well, and I liked her. And I know a bit about Kate and so I want to help out. She told me she has a friend called Barbie, and at some point I'm going to arrange a little party for the three of you. I am hoping you'll become friends. It'll help her."

Edward nodded. She watched him glance around the room still cold and failed and utterly sad to her.

"It'll be nicer when I'm done with it," she said. "Maybe a little rug and some pictures. And a lamp for the night table. Whatever she wants. Clothes. She'll need clothes, and I have a few coupons left. The wall closet has a rail and a shelf."

For a while they said nothing, then Edward stood up. "I should be going. The aerodynamics class starts in forty minutes. Thank you for the money, Dr. Giroux. I'm sure it'll all go well."

"Want me to drive you?"

"No, thank you. I came on the bicycle."

———

It was evening twilight when Claire drove out to the horse farm. On the passenger seat lay the note Kate had written two days ago. She'd meant to go there sooner, but there hadn't been a spare moment until now. At the farm she stopped the car, got out, and looked around. The main building was a traditional two-storey stone-and-brick with white shutters; not far away there was a large wooden barn and a few outbuildings. White paddock fences stretched in vanishing lines all the way to the trees, with horses in some of the paddocks. A hawk circling high above the trees.

She walked up to the main building and used the knocker on the front door. A woman opened. She was dressed in a tweed jacket and jodhpurs and riding boots. She seemed annoyed to see someone standing there.

"Yes?" she said. "I'm just on my way to the barn."

"This won't take long," said Claire. She told her who she was, and the woman said she was Mrs. Fitzhenry, the owner. Claire told her what had happened to Kate, and handed her the note. The woman looked at it.

"The poor girl," she said. "I heard about it, but I didn't know it was her house."

"She can leave the hospital in a day or two but she won't be able to work for a while."

"That's all too bad. Tell her I'm thinking of her, and I hope she gets better soon."

"I'll tell her. The thing is, she is worried about her job here. She loves it."

"I'm sure she does." Mrs. Fitzhenry stepped resolutely past Claire and pulled the door shut.

"She is looking forward to coming back," said Claire.

"Yes, of course she is. But, you see, we're very busy here, all the time, and when she didn't show up and I didn't hear from her I hired someone else. If Kate isn't absolutely fit, she's of no use to me. Horses can be dangerous."

"She wrote the note two days ago and I should have brought it out then, but there was never any time. At the moment I work extra shifts at different hospitals."

"Two days wouldn't have made any difference. The new girl started weeks ago."

"But can Kate get her situation back when she is better?"

Mrs. Fitzhenry looked at her, conflicted for a short moment only. "Let's see how it goes," she said then. "The girl we hired loves horses too. They all do. And she's good with them. But I wish Kate a speedy recovery. You can tell her that."

Next evening, after a shift from early morning till mid-afternoon, Claire brought Kate home. She kept it as simple as possible. They ate supper in the kitchen and then she ran the geyser for a sponge bath with Lifebuoy toilet soap and a fresh scrubbing towel.

Kate came out of the bathroom in a borrowed nightgown and went straight to bed and turned out the light, as if to get this day over with quickly and then hopefully to begin anew. Claire was standing in the doorway.

"I looked under the bandage in the mirror," Kate said from the dark. "The whole cheek. It's terrible."

"Not all *that* terrible, Kate. And it will get better as the swelling goes down and the redness fades. There'll be some scarring, but after a while when it's all healed we can talk to a surgeon who works on scars. It's amazing what he can do."

"I don't really know how to thank you. But *thank you*."

"You are most welcome, Kate. I want to help you, and I think we'll get used to the arrangement and to one another quickly. Tomorrow write me a list of what you need."

"All right, I'll do that. Thank you again, Claire."

Claire could tell that Kate was tearing up, and she wanted to go there and reassure her. But she didn't, so as not to intrude. She said, "I'm grateful, too, Kate. For the good company and that I'm able to help you. Sleep well." And she turned and closed the door.

For a while she stood on the landing and listened. Then she went downstairs to the living room and sat in the chair in the dark. *What have you done? What about when Thomas comes home? He never wrote back about baby William. Not a word. And now Kate. But he will like her, how could he not? We could be a family. We could.*

But behind that hope she was also worried about the change. And what if the war had made Thomas worse? All the mental cases and the traumatic injuries she was seeing among early returnees.

She put her hands on the armrests, pushed herself up, and walked to the window. The blackout curtain was gone now, but the glass still bore bits of tape that would have to be soaked off. Darkness out there. She turned away and left the room.

Eight

WHEN KATE WANTED to see what was left of her house, Claire drove her there; Kate in the passenger seat, pale and silent.

The bomb site was in the southern part of town, and Claire's house was in the southeast. Not very far away, but then nothing in Talbot was all that far away from anywhere else. Certainly not from King Street and the business area. Before the war there had been two crosstown buses, but in those days the town's population had been twenty-three thousand. Now, no one knew.

Claire turned the corner, and there it was, halfway down the street. A hoarding had been put up and a uniformed policeman stood guarding a gap in the barrier. Behind him two men were poking through the rubble.

Claire pulled over and rolled down her window. "My friend lived here," she said to the policeman. "This was her house. She wants to see if anything can be salvaged."

He bent down and looked in at Kate. The bandage on her face, the burnt hair.

"They're still making the site secure. Possible gas leaks and electrical issues. So she can't go in."

Kate climbed out and walked around the car. "I just want to see, officer," Claire heard her say to the policeman.

"You can look, but don't go in."

Kate said nothing to that and took another step.

"You can't go in, luv."

"I won't, but I need to see. Can you please move aside a bit?"

Claire watched her standing in the gap in the hoarding. Her house gone. The remains of a staircase sagging, going nowhere. Chunks of bricks and mortar, splintered floorboards, a jumble of posts and beams supporting nothing. Debris everywhere.

"Over there," Claire heard her say to the policeman. "The bit of picture frame and paper sticking up where the staircase used to be. See it? I think I recognize it. It's a watercolour. What's left of it. Can I have it?"

"A watercolour?"

"Over there." Kate pointed.

"That," said the policeman.

"Can you please ask them to bring it to me? My mother painted it."

The policeman called to the men and one of them clambered over there. He wore good black shoes and a suit and tie under his coat. He freed the item and picked it up, shook off some loose shards from the broken frame, and brought it over. The policeman took it and handed it to her. "Careful now," Claire heard him say. "There's still that bit of glass in it."

Kate thanked him and put the picture on the back seat.

On the way home Kate asked Claire to drive along King Street, and at one point asked her to slow down and then to stop.

"I won't be long." She pushed open the door and climbed out.

Claire watched her cross the street, stopping in the middle for a lorry to pass but then the lorry stopped for her and an arm came out the window and waved her on.

Shops all along here, too many of them failed and boarded up. Another bomb site. On the other side of the street, in front of his tea room, the proprietor in his little white apron was carrying a tray. Two of the small tables were occupied. People sitting in the mild March sun with their coats unbuttoned, sipping tea in silence.

She cranked down the window and looked around. She loved this town. Had loved it ever since she came back from Montreal years ago, leaving her mother to her ill-fated adventures.

Across the street the proprietor noticed Kate. He set down his tray on a table and quickly stepped into the street and offered her his arm to help her across. He seemed to know her well.

They stood talking and he was visibly shocked by what he heard. More was said and then Kate turned and pointed at the car, and the proprietor looked and nodded at Claire. She nodded back.

The proprietor stepped into his shop and was gone for a moment while Kate waited. He came back and handed her something small. She closed her hand over it. They said a few more words, then Kate turned and crossed the street again and came back to the car.

"What was that all about?" said Claire.

"Tony is a friend of David's. I lost something in the house and he replaced it for me."

"Replaced what?"

Claire waited a while and when Kate did not answer she let it go.

At home they brought what was left of the picture up to Kate's room. "One day," said Claire, "when there is such a thing as picture glass again, we can get it framed and glassed in. Even with some of it missing."

"Maybe. It's fine for now."

There was a small nail already in the wall where the crib had stood; Kate eased the paper out of the remains of the frame, poked the nail through the top of the paper, and hung it there.

"I knew your mother painted," said Claire. "But I never saw any of her work. This is nice. Sunflowers."

"She used to go on outings with her painting group. At one time she told me she did it to keep sane. I think she always regretted giving up her job when I was born and they moved here."

Claire nodded. She knew that. Mary had told her.

"Those men at the bomb site," said Kate. "Making sure the place is safe after all this time? That's what the town does as soon as possible after a bomb. Not weeks later. I've seen them do it. Men in coveralls and work boots, not in suits. So who were those two, and what were they looking for?"

Nine

ON THE SATURDAY of the garden party Kate asked Claire if the bandages around her chest could perhaps come off now. They sat in the kitchen over tea and toast; breakfast, lunch, or tea, it was hard to say. It was three in the afternoon; Claire had come home close to eight in the morning and then slept for a few hours.

"How is the pain when you breathe in?"

"Almost gone," said Kate. "I'd love to breathe in deeply once in a while, but I can't because of the bandage. My cheek too. Can we look at it?"

"Yes, of course. And, yes, I think we can try it without the bandage. Once it's off don't lift anything heavy for a while longer, and if you want to breathe deeply do it slowly. In stages."

In the bathroom Kate stood with her arms up while Claire unpinned the Tensor bandage and unwound it coil by coil.

"There. How does that feel?"

Kate took a cautious deep breath and smiled. "Much better."

The injury on her cheek was next. She stood in front of the mirror while the tape came off, pulling at her skin and revealing the injury inch by inch.

Her cheek looked terrible.

Behind her, Claire said, "It's not too bad. What do you think?"

"Oh, Claire. Look at it."

"It's still a bit swollen, and the stitches pull. But I can see that they're ready to come out. Then it'll soon look much better. If you like we can take them out now. Might as well."

Kate raised her hand and touched her cheek with her fingertips. The new her. Clearly marked. The injury was wide in places, narrow in others, all somehow pulled together with black thread and with scar tissue forming.

"Were there bits missing?"

"Of tissue? Yes. Whatever piece of shrapnel or masonry did that, travelled with enormous energy and speed. Luckily it just grazed you. Come. Sit down and let's do the stitches now."

Claire went to the first aid cabinet and came back with alcohol, wipes, scissors, and tweezers.

"Turn the cheek to the light and hold very still. And just so you know, before we have the party I want to tell you that you're still shouting a bit. Maybe you're just used to it by now, so let's try something. Count to ten for me and as you do, lower your voice in stages."

She did, and at number five Claire raised a finger, smiled and said, "Perfect. Try it. Say a few sentences at that level and listen to it inside your head."

The tea party took place in the gazebo at the back of the garden. Kate had never seen it.

Her long-time friend Barbie had come, and they hugged carefully. "I'm sorry to see you like this, kid. Dr. Giroux told me a bit of what happened to you. I had no idea."

"I couldn't tell you. I was in the hospital."

A young man was there as well. "Edward," he said, and shook her hand. In the garden Claire led the way, parting bushes and bending branches like a jungle explorer, and suddenly there was the gazebo. Her tree house, Claire called it. A delicate wooden structure, a hexagon, two sides enclosed with tongue-and-groove, all painted white. A crab apple tree stood next to it, leaning on it and overhanging it, branches full of pink blossoms against the blue sky.

There was no furniture, and so they sat on the wood floor around a tablecloth with tea and lemonade and pre-war Dare biscuits from Claire's secret stash. Not far away they could see ducks landing on a bomb crater that had filled with water.

Claire talked to them about the importance of kindness and friendship, especially in these times, these last months of the war in England, she said, when the war had essentially been won but the damage done by it, even in victory, to the nation and to people was still sinking in. And as Kate's story showed, the terror was not over yet.

They listened to her and nodded, munching biscuits and stealing glances at one another. Kate had a slightly smaller bandage on her cheek, and she could tell that Barbie and Edward were trying not to stare at it or at the wild haircut she'd given herself last night around the places where her hair had caught fire and was now growing in.

"I'll have to go to work soon," Claire said to them. "But you stay and enjoy this. Take your time. Get to know each other, and you girls get re-acquainted. If you like, this can be *your* tree house now. Your special place where you can meet and tell each other about yourselves."

They were much the same age: twenty-four she and Barbie, and twenty-five Edward. Barbie, with her beautiful dark hair and no scars anywhere, told them that for sixpence an hour she worked at a charity shop. And on Saturday nights she put on a gown they gave her and sat in the display window at Arlington's, the piano shop on Sutton Street, and played a Steinway baby grand. The owners had hired her temporarily because business was so poor. The hope was that people walking by would stop to look in and listen, and one day they'd come back and buy something.

KURT PALKA

"I'll come and listen," said Kate, and Edward said he'd come too. "We can go together," he said to Kate.

They sipped tea and ate biscuits and became more and more relaxed with one another. They looked around at all the trees, at the graceful little shelter they were in. "Our tree house," said Barbie, and then she said that if Kate wanted to talk about what had happened to her, that would be great, but if she didn't that would be fine as well.

"I don't mind telling you," said Kate. And she told them about the bomb and her mother and aunt, and her injuries. The bandages around her cracked ribs had come off only today, and now she'd have to learn to breathe normally again. She'd lost strength, and in the mornings and at the end of a day her body still hurt.

She touched her hair and said she'd tried to even it out, but it grew in strangely.

"What do you think?" she asked them. But then quickly she said, "Don't tell me. I know. And I don't care. No, that's not true. Of course I care. I was going to have it fixed by a colleague at Paramedics. She used to do my hair and she was good at it. One and six for a shampoo and cut. But there've been changes and she was posted to another district. And the gash in my cheek is from a fragment during the explosion. Claire says it'll look better eventually, and she also knows a surgeon who specializes in fixing scars." She paused. "Am I shouting? Today she told me that sometimes I'm still shouting a bit, since the bomb. Am I shouting now?"

"No, you're not," said Edward. "Your voice is perfectly normal. It's the same level as ours."

"Good." She smiled at him. At least she was alive, she said, while her mother and aunt were dead, and David had gone missing on his last foreign assignment.

"I knew them," Barbie said to Edward. "And I liked them. Her mother painted and David was a professor at St. Anne's. A good one. I once took a course with him."

Kate told them that she saw him in her dreams, going past on a bicycle, an old black Raleigh with a pedal that made a regular clanking noise against the chain guard. Pedalling past, he'd turn to her and smile.

"There was a good doctor whom I saw a long time ago," she said. "He helped me a lot. When my dad got killed and I felt guilty, he came up with the idea of ambulance training. And one day he told me that nobody can 'keep it all together,' as he called it. You know, being still and sure inside. Nobody could do that all the time. Not I, not he, nobody. We can get it together for moments and maybe even for hours, but keeping it together throughout the day, day after day, is something else entirely. And hardly anybody can do that, he told me. But it's a worthwhile goal."

When she said that, the other two glanced at each other. She saw that. She caught that exchange and wondered about it. But not too much; she was grateful that they were here and accepted her, even in her sorry state. She changed her position and tried to take a deep breath but had to stop halfway. She saw them noticing.

"I was very fit once," she said. "But the bomb did a lot of damage to me. Inside and out. I know that, and I'm working on it. At Paramedics we did practice races with loaded stretchers and we worked out with sandbags. And I rode horses. David got me into that. He was born on a horse farm in Nova Scotia, in Canada."

"*Paramedics*," said Edward. "That's it! I thought I remembered you from somewhere. You drove a big Bedford ambulance truck and you wore a uniform."

"I did. I'm a certified paramedic technician. I loved that job and the teamwork."

She told them that at the moment she wasn't working at anything. Couldn't, really. And she missed it very much. She described to them what it had been like to drive an ambulance truck after an air raid—the adrenaline rush, the closeness with your colleagues, and the fierce resolve never to give in to fear, never, never. Digging people out of the smoking rubble of bomb sites, and day after day the importance of emergency care and of speed, with the wounded in the back of the truck. And on the worst days the unbearable stillness of a dead child.

They sat and listened, spellbound. They looked at her eyes and not once at her hair or her cheek, looked at her as though they were seeing her differently suddenly, or in a different light.

Barbie said, "That was the first time I heard you really talking about it."

"I know. I did talk about it, but only with colleagues. My mother never knew any of the details, not really, but David knew. He was easy to talk to. He knew not to say anything. Just to listen. But with him you knew he understood and it went to the right place."

She turned to Edward. "And you?"

"Wow," he said. "After all this . . . I don't know." But he told them that after technical school he'd begun working at the Royal Canadian Air Force base not far away, and now he attended courses that earned him credits toward his further career training in aviation. He said that becoming a pilot without having gone to the academy was the hard way. But it had been done before, and it was what he wanted more than anything else. He said that twice; *more than anything else.*

After a moment of silence between them Barbie said, "Talking about what we all want—I just want to become a good pianist. Really good. But I have this job, too, and perhaps I'm too old already, but I don't want to think that and, anyway, it doesn't stop me from wanting it. More than anything else, too."

They nodded at that, then Edward said, "Kate, if you're looking for work, there might be a job open at the mill. I worked there, but when I signed up for the aerodynamics course I had to give it up."

"What sort of job?" Kate remembered him too now, from somewhere, vaguely. The war had made them all grow up in a hurry. A good face on him. Brown eyes and a nice smile.

"Raking the grate at the millrun," he said. "It's not hard, and the money is the usual. Sixpence an hour."

"I think it'll be too hard for her," said Barbie. "Lifting that heavy rake full of leaves and stuff."

"She doesn't have to *lift* it, just drag it up. And she can choose how much to fill the rake."

"I can try," said Kate. "I could use the money. I lost my handbag with my purse and everything else in it in the bombing. All my savings. It's down there somewhere under all that rubble. Paramedics was paying me for a while longer, but less and less, and now it stopped altogether."

Not long after that Edward said he had to get back to the base. They put the dishes into the basket, and Edward and Barbie took turns carrying the basket and Kate carried the tablecloth. On the way through the trees and bushes she fell behind, and when she caught up again she heard Edward say to Barbie that even with her chopped-off hair and the bandaged cheek, or perhaps all the more because of it and maybe set off by it all, he thought her face was nice. And there was something interesting about her. Something wild in her eyes, the way she looked at you. He wondered what would become of her, with her injuries and her family all gone.

Ten

CLAIRE LOVED seeing Kate getting stronger and more certain. Calmer. The injury was not healed enough yet for the plastic surgeon, but it was coming along. There were two scars that crossed, and there was scar tissue in the upper and lower fields of the X. Claire could see that Kate was self-conscious about it, and she tried to reassure her.

Because of her irregular schedule the kitchen had become their meeting ground. Kate prepared meals and often they ate at three or four in the morning; sometimes they had breakfast at noon. While Claire was at work, Kate stood in line to do the shopping, and she planted a victory garden where she grew vegetables.

Each week they had at least three good sit-down sessions. Whatever the time of day or night, they would sit at the oil-cloth-covered table against the wall by the window, and they would have a meal or just sip tea, and talk. There was so much to talk about.

Claire could tell that the tea party in the tree house had been successful; friendships had been formed and renewed, and Kate and Edward had been at Arlington's twice already to hear Barbie play. Apparently Barbie liked classical music the most, but she also liked traditional songs and the wartime songs, and the American music that could be heard on AFN Radio.

Kate had described to Claire how on some evenings the three of them met in the church basement, where there was a room with chairs and an old upright piano. Barbie had permission from the sexton to use that piano for practice, and when the three of them were there, Barbie played and they all sang along happily—songs like "The Bonnie Banks o' Loch Lomond" and "The Rose of Tralee," Kate's mother's favourite, or "Carrickfergus": *I wish I was in Carrickfergus, only for nights in Ballygrand . . .*

At one of their sit-downs in the kitchen, Kate asked her why she never played the piano that stood in a corner of the living room.

"Because I wouldn't know how," Claire admitted. "I never learned to play any musical instrument."

"Really? So the poor piano never gets used. It just sits there?"

"It's a beautiful piece of furniture," said Claire. "And it has a long history. It was practically hand-built by my mother, maybe thirty years ago in France. One day you'll meet her. She inherited the piano factory where I grew up. During the Great War. Before we moved to England and then to Canada." She smiled at Kate. "There is lots I haven't told you yet."

"You moved to England with a piano?"

"Oh, no. Only with what we could carry. I was maybe nine years old."

"And the piano?"

"My mother found it here, and bought it."

"And now the poor thing never gets used? In that case do you think you could lend it to Barbie for a while, so that she has a good piano to practise on at home? Rather than the old wreck at the church."

"Now, slow down, Kate. Slow down. Lend my Molnar to Barbie? I never even heard her play. Is she any good?"

"I think she's very good, and she's really working on it. She's been playing for years and she's taking advanced classes. Her mother pays for half of them and Barbie pays the rest. From her shop job."

"Her mother helps out? What does her mother do?"

"Works in a foundry for one pound ten a week, welding stabilizers onto bombs."

"A foundry."

"Yes. I'm sure Barbie would be careful with the piano. Her stint at Arlington's is coming to an end, and the piano at the church is old and rickety. Barbie says the action is all worn out. And there are mice down there."

"Hmm. Let me think about it."

A few days later she told Kate that she'd like to hear Barbie play. Not on the Molnar, but on the piano at the church. And not popular music. Something classical. Beethoven, if possible.

They were all there that evening: Barbie and her mother, Edward, Kate, and Claire. The church basement was a dim, eerie place filled with strange shapes under dust covers. Baited mouse traps sat along walls, and the only light came from four bulbs on the ceiling and from the two small windows high up in the street-side wall. They could see people's feet walking by on the pavement.

Claire found a chair, wiped it off, and arranged herself on it. She watched Barbie sit down on the piano stool and sit there for a moment with her head down and her hands in her lap. Then she raised her hands and began to play "Für Elise."

Claire listened. After a while she leaned back with her eyes closed, and then for long moments it was to her as though the room were filling with the pure, silken air through the open window above the mill brook in Montmagny, and with the soft light of her childhood there, and the music, that fine work so nicely played, stirred something deep inside her, long forgotten. Dinner was over and the green couch stood against the wall and

Xavier was sitting on that couch, listening to her mother's exquisite phrasing at the piano, and even though the war was on, Xavier was making them feel safe and the music and the air and the light through the window were so very unforgettable. Next she had been sent upstairs to her room but her mother was still playing the piano and she opened the door just a bit to listen and . . . not yet, not yet. Please keep playing . . .

When Barbie had finished, Claire sat with her eyes closed for a moment longer as the dream faded. Then she stood up and thanked Barbie and applauded. She felt sad and nostalgic and happy at once, and she made no attempt to hide how much she was moved by the experience.

On the way home she told Kate that yes, she would lend Barbie the Molnar.

"*Lend*, mind you," she said. "Let's say for six months for now. To be renewed if all goes well."

"Great. I'll tell her."

"You can also tell her that I'll arrange to have it tuned and moved to their house as soon as I can find suitable transport. It'll have to be something on rubber tires, with the proper equipment to hoist the piano safely up and down."

Eleven

"KATE HENDERSON!" said Dr. Elliott in the hallway at Riverdale. "How are you, Kate? Dr. Giroux told me about everything that's happened to you. I was very sorry to hear it."

"Thank you, Dr. Elliott." She shifted the fifteen-pound sandbag she was carrying into her other arm.

"What brings you here?"

"I've just been to see the area supervisor at Paramedics to ask about coming back to work. I think I'm fit enough by now to help out. Maybe not to drive a truck or carry stretchers, but with other things."

"And what did she say?"

"That she thinks it's too soon. She lent me this exercise bag to work out with. We did that regularly when I was here."

From the disappointment just now her breath came short and shallow. She knew he could tell and she tried to calm herself and to breathe more deeply and slowly.

He looked at the sandbag in the crook of her arm, looked at her face. At the bandage.

"Kate," he said. "Shall we go and talk for a minute?" He waited, and when she nodded yes, he turned and led the way. In his office he waved her towards the chairs in the corner.

"Do you and Dr. Giroux find time to talk? I know she works long hours."

"We do have our sit-downs. Often in the early mornings. When I hear her come home I get up and then we sit in the kitchen and have a meal. And sometimes before she leaves. Claire is my bright spot. She is wonderful. So easy to talk to."

"Your bright spot," he said. "And the dark spots?"

"Empty places, Dr. Elliott. People I loved are suddenly gone. Some days I feel I've lost my bearing because they were strong and dependable. And sometimes I think that entire pieces of me went missing along the way."

He nodded and took his time with that. Then he said, "They would have, Kate. When we lose people we love, parts of ourselves are lost with them. When they are gone we can see what they meant to us. We like the way we were with them, how they made us feel, and we love them even more. And that love grows and it never goes away. It becomes a strong part of us, the memory of their love for us and ours for them. In that way they never leave us. Talk to me, Kate."

But she couldn't just yet. She feared her voice might fail her. It was always kindness that moved her the most. To escape for a moment she looked around his office, a place she had good memories of. The dark-green shade of the desk lamp was still the same. As was the way he took his time and sat back in his chair, not behind his desk but in the corner with her, by the window. The blinds were down and the light was soft.

"Kate," he said. "Why didn't you ever come and see me? Since losing your mother and aunt? And the bomb and your injury. That must have all been very difficult."

She looked at him and her eyes stung. She looked away.

"Some days it's worse," she said then. "Like today. But on other days I feel that I am learning to deal with it."

"Good, Kate. Good. It comes and goes in waves, but we get better at navigating those waves. I think you are as strong inside as ever. And courageous. Today, coming in and asking for work, and now, sitting here and telling me. Sometimes we don't know what's next, especially in these times. But what's next will show itself. It always does. And there is strength in patience. Would you like some tea?"

She shook her head. "No, thank you. I should be going."

"Do you still need that bandage, Kate? Your cheek is healed, isn't it?"

"It is, but . . ."

"Is it the scar?"

"Yes. Some days I hate it. Like today. So I cover it up. There's a part-time job at the mill that I'm going to apply for this afternoon."

"Good. What kind of job?"

"Raking the grate at the weir. I may not be able to do it."

"But you can try."

"If they let me."

She stood up, then hesitated. The doctor was watching her closely. He stood up too, went to his desk and picked up one of his cards and handed it to her. "Anytime, Kate. I mean it. Anytime at all."

At the mill, the manager heard her out and he looked at her standing there in front of his desk. He leaned forward and put his elbow down and said for her to try and arm-wrestle him. She sat down on the chair and reached for his hand. It was big and rough, and she leaned into it with all her strength, trying to bend it to the desk, but it was impossible. He sat calmly looking at her straining, and he took his time studying her face and her hair and the bandage. Then he said, "All right, all right. You can let go. Not bad. What's under the bandage?"

"An injury from when our house was bombed. It's mostly healed. My ribs are much better, too, and the hair is growing in. Before all that I worked as a certified paramedic and I drove an ambulance truck."

"Your house was bombed?"

"Yes. Back in February."

"Can you peel the bandage back a bit? Let's see. All closed, is it, no open wound?"

"No." She lifted the tape. "In a few days I'm seeing a surgeon. He works on scars, and when he's done it'll hopefully look much better."

He looked at her cheek and read her expression, and he took his time. Then he said, "So come back when the surgery is done and it's all healed again. You can have the job. Not the raking job, something else. Wait here."

He got up and walked to the door, a big man in a coverall and a harness belt with the carabiner dangling. Minutes later he was back with another big man whom he introduced as the shed boss, and the shed boss told her to come along and he'd show her what her job would be.

It was shifting transmission gears according to turbine pressures, oiling bearings with a long-spout machinist's oil can, and servicing grease nipples with a pedal pump that she would have to drag around on wheels.

"Just stay clear of the belts," he said to her. "I've seen them do serious damage. It's Kate, right?"

"Right."

"So get yourself straightened out, Kate, and come back when you're ready. The boss says the job is yours. Twenty hours a week, he'll give you. Sixpence an hour. You'll get a boiler suit and a cap and gloves, and when you start you can follow me around for a while and I'll show you the ropes. All right?"

She walked back to Claire's house, elated. The area supervisor didn't want her, and Mrs. Fitzhenry didn't want her, but at the mill they did. She had a paying job! Claire would be home soon and she couldn't wait to tell her.

Three days later she sat tilted back in an examination chair, under a light too bright to open her eyes, while the surgeon was poking at her cheek.

"Hmm," he said. "I think we'll be all right. You want to see this, Dr. Giroux? Most of the scar tissue—this and this—we can remove it and tighten up. She's young and her skin is still soft and flexible, and it'll stretch and relax and fill in again. At first it'll pull a bit, but that'll pass. After a while it should all be just fine lines."

"When can you do it?" said Claire. "Soon?"

"I don't know about *soon*. But talk to the nurse. Maybe she can find an opening."

The nurse did find an opening, and next afternoon already Kate sat in that tilt-back chair again, with the bright light beaming down. The sedation and local anaesthesia made it all far removed, and eventually she lost track of time and even of where she was and what was being done to her. Later the nurse asked her to stand up and take a few steps. They were just the two of them in the room now.

"He's an artist, Dr. Shaw is," said the nurse. "Just a few fine lines, you'll see. Come, let's walk a bit. Get your balance back. Take my arm. Left foot first."

Twelve

CLAIRE WAITED IN FRONT of her friend Annabelle's office building on Whitehall, and at the appointed time Annabelle, in what she called her Whitehall uniform of dark greys, a white blouse, and sensible shoes, arrived and shepherded her in by the main entrance, past security. The guard looked at Annabelle's pass and nodded. He had Claire fill out a form and sign it, then he asked her to empty her handbag onto a wooden tray, where he pushed her things about with a pointed finger. He thanked her and waved her on.

They walked down the hall and up the wide stone stairs. In her office, Annabelle dialled the operator and gave her code and asked for the call to be timed because the caller would be paying for it. She gave the operator the number of Claire's mother in Nova Scotia, then handed the receiver to Claire and left the room.

Claire waited through the clicks and then she heard her mother say hello.

"It's Claire, Maman. Can you hear me?"

"Claire! How lovely. Yes, I can hear you. Where are you?"

"I am in a friend's office. Annabelle Spencer. I must have mentioned her to you. We met at university and now she works for the government. I have a question for you: do you remember Captain Xavier Boucher?"

There was a silence, then her mother said, "Yes, of course I do. I'll never forget that man, Claire."

"You used to play 'Für Elise' for him, and 'Moonlight Sonata,' back in Montmagny during the Great War, and he showed me 'Tous mes animaux,' the finger shadow game, and we played ball in the parlour because I wasn't allowed to go outside and—"

"Slow down, Claire. I have a hard time understanding you. What's this all about?"

She took a deep breath and closed her eyes for a moment.

"Is this about Montmagny?" said her mother. "And about Xavier? They were difficult times, Claire. I know how you felt about him; you told me later in Montreal, when he died. We were sitting on the bench in front of the hospital."

"I remember that too. Except I had somehow forgotten it, or misplaced it, or the war overshadowed it. But last week something happened that brought it all back to me."

"What happened, Claire? Are you well? Is everything all right? Are you still working those long hours? Are you safe?"

"Safe? Yes, more or less. And, yes, I am still working long hours, but by choice. The war is practically over and our soldiers are starting to come home. The Canadian ones must be as well. Thomas should be home soon too."

"*Thomas.*"

"My husband."

"I know too well who Thomas is. If I never—"

"Not now, Maman. Please."

"All right. So what happened last week?"

"I sat in a church basement while a young woman, dark-haired and beautiful like you back then, played 'Für Elise' on a very old Chickering. And suddenly it was like a dream. It took me right back to Montmagny and I could see the special light from the window, and Xavier sat on the green couch in the living room and you were playing 'Für Elise.' Next I'd been sent upstairs to bed but I could still hear you playing. You played it so very well, Maman, with such fine phrasing. I used to get out of bed and open the door a crack to listen. And I knew then, I could tell from the way you were playing, that you loved him. The war was on and we were living on scraps from their field kitchen while he stayed at our house. Their wounded were all over the factory grounds and the dead lay piled up by the willows. But you loved him and I did too. I was maybe seven years old, and I did not understand because Dad had died less than two years before that. And we had loved him too. Very much."

For a long moment there was a silence on the phone, just a rush of static, perhaps the transatlantic cable stirring on the ocean floor across all that distance.

"Maman," she said. "Are you there?"

"Three years, Claire. Yes, I am here. I'm just—I am moved. Your father had died three years before that, not less than two, as you say. Three unbelievably horrible years. And they weren't scraps from their field kitchen but decent meals. Considering. And you were eight years old, not seven, and it was very important for us to keep up our spirits. Xavier ate with us, and for our meals I always put out a tablecloth and linen napkins, and even if it was only turnips and bits of horse meat, or just turnips and potatoes, we ate from good dinner plates with my mother's silverware."

Claire was silent for a while, then she said, "Yes. I remember that too now. I'm sorry."

"There's nothing to be sorry about, Claire. It's all right. Sometimes we need to be reminded. Of details, but of the context, too."

"I just wanted to tell you that whatever I said that day on the bench at Sainte Mère de Dieu about you and Xavier, it was probably all wrong and inappropriate. I did not understand it myself, but when I heard 'Für Elise' again it became so very clear to me. The context, as you say, our situation. *Your* situation. How difficult it must have been and what you must have been going through. I was too young then, but last week in that church basement I suddenly understood. That's what I wanted to say, Maman. Mostly that. That's why I wanted to call you."

More silence on the telephone, then her mother said, "That man saved me, Claire. He saved both of us, even though he was with us for less than a year. He was life and kindness. He was hope. He was someone to love, Claire. In all that darkness and horror. Anyway, thank you, for saying it. Thank you. It's all a very long time ago."

Annabelle came back into the room, smiled and pointed at her watch.

Claire nodded. "My friend's just back, Maman, and I shouldn't tie up this phone much longer. I'll write to you. But I'll tell you quickly that I've taken in a bright young woman. Her father is dead and a bomb fell on her house and killed her mother and aunt. I knew her mother quite well."

"You took her in?"

"Yes. I'm hoping that when Thomas comes back the three of us can be like a family. I like her very much and I think he'll like her too. How could he not?"

There was a lengthy silence.

Then her mother said, "Just be happy, Claire. Please be happy. And come and visit me sometime. Can you?"

In the car on the way back to Great Maze Pond and Guy's Hospital it was difficult not to think back to the arguments with her mother about Thomas. Not at first; early on her mother had quite liked him. At least she said she did. One summer,

more than halfway through medical school, they spent two
weeks in Nova Scotia, and Thomas met everyone there: Mother
and Mr. Chandler, Mildred at the hotel, and Father William.

She remembered it clearly. His confusing power over her.
His hands that she'd first noticed when he'd held the door open
for her at study hall. His right hand on the bronze bar, a strong
hand, well defined, and the knuckles pronounced, the tendons
and muscles clenching the fingers around the bar. She could
have named every bone and tendon and every muscle in that
hand, had isolated them and stripped them out of cadavers and
made precise drawings of them for exams. And here they were
in real life and her intimate knowledge of them made them all
the more interesting because these were full of purpose, and
they were strong and capable. Potentially dangerous too, unless
one was their friend.

So strange. And later his eyes across the library table. Black
like coal and mysterious, and not one glimmer in them because
the ceiling lights could not reach them. Good-looking. Dark-
brown wavy hair, a handsome face, and a smile it was hard to
look away from. They couldn't talk and so he scribbled notes
and passed them across the table. He sent four notes before
she finally replied with one. Which was only a question mark,
but it was the thin edge.

That summer in Saint Homais they stayed in the loft high
up in the church annex, a room she remembered so well from
years ago, and sometimes in her nights she stood at the window

and could see her future as she wanted it to be: she, a medical doctor with her own practice and a family. Two children and Thomas, her loving husband, successful in his profession as well, all kept safe and contained in a half-timbered house in Talbot, the lovely small town she'd discovered not far from London. It had a hospital and a college that attracted foreign students, and its history went back all the way to the Romans, when it served as a garrison and horse-changing station on the river.

She was doing well at med school, and he was her brilliant and demanding lover, like a secret addiction who only had to look at her in a certain way and she'd want him. Her fiancé, she called him. He was jealous and twice started fights with students who he thought were paying too much attention to her. He was also falling behind in his studies, and was beginning to hint at the possibility that he might change direction. Too much math in engineering; he might drop out and do something more immediately useful, such as join the military.

One morning in the Saint Homais kitchen, from around the corner to the cold room, she overheard Mr. Chandler say to her mother, "Hélène, the man has a temper. I noticed it yesterday when I showed him around the shop. He picked up a tool and dropped it, and for a moment there was something, a sudden change of mood, an instant hot anger like a flipped switch. And I thought . . . Shh."

He must have heard her, some small sound, and he said no more.

She closed the cold-room door and stepped around the corner and said, "I know that, Maman. Thomas does have a little temper, but he's aware of it and he's learning to control it. I can help him with it. I can handle it. There's something good and strong about him, and I want you both to know that I love him and that this is nothing."

In looking back, so naïve, so touching. But also positive and self-confident.

Next time in Saint Homais, in the summer of 1939, she was there alone. She had her medical degree and was married but had kept her professional name. And she was happily pregnant with their first child. Thomas had signed up and been sent to basic training and then on an advanced course; he'd just been enlisted as a sergeant. She spent time with her mother, slept in the church annex again, and went for long walks along the shore. When Mother asked about Thomas and her marriage she never said much. She didn't say that, yes, there had been arguments, and once in a while a raised hand followed by apologies. Instead she said that, with the war coming, times were difficult and they had to get used to each other, but she was happy. Did he have family, Mother wanted to know, and Claire told her that his mother had died years ago and that he had no contact with his father. Mother looked at her in that certain way, and never asked again.

A few weeks later, when Claire was back in England, there came the news that Germany had invaded Poland, and World War II had broken out.

September 1939. And in all the time since then he'd been home only once, a few months after the stillbirth; a sad and hopeful and confusing seven days of frequent air raid alarms and bombardments; of rushes of anger and a raised hand once for which he apologized, and much guilty, confused love-making. After that she'd never heard from him again. Not once. Not even when she wrote to tell him about little William.

She shifted down, turned the last corner, and pulled into the car park at Guy's. There. Locked the car and slung the strap of her handbag over her shoulder and entered the building by the main entrance. She liked this. Felt confident and at home here in her milieu. The narrow green corridors deep in the building used as air raid shelters during the Blitz. Familiar faces. Everyone knowing her, nodding and saying her name in passing. *Dr. Giroux.*

Thirteen

FOUR DAYS LATER, in the early hours of Tuesday, May 8, 1945, Claire was halfway through her shift at Riverdale when the intercom clicked on and the voice of Marjorie in the front office said: "HEAR THIS, HEAR THIS, EVERYONE: GERMANY HAS SURRENDERED! THE WAR IS OVER! IT'S OVER, DEAR PEOPLE. HALLELUJAH! IT'S OVER! HALLELUJAH!" They could hear Marjorie laughing as she put the speaker on the hook and disconnected.

That day Claire drove home with all the windows down. She had to go slowly because everywhere people were dancing in the streets, waving newspapers and laughing and hugging each other and holding up two fingers in the victory sign. On King Street loudspeakers had been set up broadcasting the BBC news and celebratory music:

Land of Hope and Glory,
Mother of the Free,

How shall we extol thee,
Who are born of thee?

She came home to find Kate working out with her sandbag on the flagstone patch near the stone angel. Kate clearly knew already; she put the sandbag down, raised her arms, and did a little dance. They hugged and laughed, and then they got into the car and drove around, honking the horn. People climbed onto the running boards and held on and waved and called out to one another.

There was only a small bandage on Kate's cheek now; the stitches were to come out in a day or two and then she'd start her mill job. She was looking forward to it.

Then the men began coming home in numbers, and many things changed. Some got better, some got worse. Most women who'd worked shifts in factories and had kept their children safe and fed during the danger years now had to hand over their jobs to men.

Barbie's mother lost her welding job at the foundry, and the next time Kate inquired about work at Paramedics, even just part-time work, the area supervisor told her they were hiring only returning soldiers now. Under her breath she added, "At twice our pay," but aloud she said that after what the men had been through it was only right to help them out. She herself would have her job only for another month while she was training someone who'd last worked at a field hospital in France.

But among the returning soldiers there were also many who were not able to work, and not just from physical injuries: a war-related mental trauma that people called war neurosis, or simply "the horrors," was beginning to be seen as a common medical condition.

In and around Talbot, men suffering from it were sent to the Riverdale psychiatric ward, where Dr. Elliott, under whom Claire had studied the psychological aspects of wound trauma, was in charge. More serious cases were sent to Scarborough Manor in London.

Barbie's brother came home and he was all right, but Edward's father, who'd been an army chaplain, did not come home. Dead from a gunshot wound in the last weeks of the war.

Claire spoke to Edward's mother and expressed her sorrow, and the woman said that they'd already sent her Walter's chaplain's badge, his watch, his wallet, and his ring.

"*Gave his life*," she said. "The notice they sent me, what nonsense. His life was took from him. He didn't *give* it. Snatched away, it was, and wasted. Just like that."

She said she'd wound the watch and held it close to her ear, and wept to hear it tick. She kept it under her pillow for three days and nights, and on the fourth day she set it to the town clock and then gave it to Edward. The badge as well. Her boy was all she had now, she said, and he was a good boy.

"But look at him, Dr. Giroux. Wanting to be a military pilot. What's wrong with them, I ask you. Will they never learn?"

When Edward showed them his dad's badge and the watch, the three of them were sitting on the floor in the tree house as usual. Eddie passed the little enamelled pin to them and let them hold it; a Maltese cross within a wreath, and the words IN THIS SIGN CONQUER were set in a circle around the centre.

A good dad, his father had been, Edward said. Strict but also kind, and never unreasonable. And it was then that Edward showed them the watch. Like a special treat. He unbuckled it carefully from his wrist and shined it on his sleeve; his dad's Broad Arrow timepiece. He let them hold it and listen to it. Watching them for their reactions, he looked lost and close to tears.

Kate had never seen him like that. She handed the watch back to him, then she got up onto her knees and moved over there and gave him a hug, with her good cheek against his.

She loved this moment, when she had an excuse to hold him close, put her arms around him and feel him breathe, feel his strong back and arms, and his troubled emotions. She'd always liked Edward, but at that moment her heart opened to him wide and she thought that if he wanted her, she could love him for the rest of her life.

That night in the kitchen she said all that to Claire, used those very words, *could love him for the rest of my life, Claire*. And she said more, shared it all in a happy rush. She could tell that Edward liked her. Had liked her all along. She knew that, and she was thankful for it. When he looked at her, she could see a light in his eyes and she loved that light.

Claire was listening closely; Kate could tell. At one point, at the words *could love him for the rest of my life*, Claire's expression changed to a fleeting recognition and a sadness, a sorrow, but in the end she smiled and nodded. She said, "I'm happy for you, Kate," and she reached and touched her hand on the table.

She was working at her mill job by then. Her boss was called Trevor, like her father, and even though this Trevor looked nothing like her dad, she liked having someone by that name back in her life. He was a good boss; strong and fair and clear in his instructions. On her first day she'd still been wearing a bandage for protection, and he'd asked her to lift it to let him see that her cheek was healed.

"Good," he said. "So put on your suit and your cap and gloves, and let me know when you're ready."

She followed him from station to station, watched him closely and then copied his actions. Shifting the transmission gears was a bit like shifting up or down in an ambulance truck, and she had to listen for the whine and the strain on the gears and pick the right moment. The grease nipples were a challenge, and she'd have to learn to clip the nozzle on tight so that the grease didn't squeeze out. Even oiling bearings with what Trevor called the spit can was tricky at first; not too much, not too little, but she'd learn.

"All right then?" Trevor said at the end of their round. "Any questions, just ask."

Fourteen

AT THE END OF MAY, Thomas came home on a medical discharge from an army hospital. As Claire would eventually find out, he'd been a platoon leader in North Africa; he'd been wounded and patched up and eventually sent back into battle with his men in Italy, and wounded again. It was never clear what he experienced in the war before or after his injuries, but within days of his homecoming he developed the now familiar nightmares and the screams and the fits.

There were numerous small, half-healed wounds to his arms and legs and back, and she wanted to see them and help him with them, but he pushed her away, hard. Once he even raised his hand at her again, but then his eyes went very round and he stopped.

There was no intimacy and none of the closeness she had been yearning for. He did not respond to her questions and he did not talk. Instead he would sit for hours with his hands clamped over his ears, and his eyes shut tight.

One week after he came home the assaults began; not on Claire, but on Kate. At first he repeatedly raised his hand at her and shouted at her to go away and who was she anyway, following him around when he didn't want her there. Then one night he dragged her from her bed onto the landing and he slapped her in the face with his big hands, left and right, finding openings around her raised forearms until Claire intervened, and then he hit her as well. He hit her harder, with ever more anger. Or perhaps with shame and self-contempt, as Claire had learned from Dr. Elliott. The shame and self-contempt of some men for what they had found out about themselves in the war, had done in the war, or had seen done by others and had not interfered. So how could they come back now to live among normal people again, and sleep in one bed with their wives who longed to be loved and held, but who would soon realize that their longings would never be fulfilled?

He was crying by then, and in a shocking scene never to be forgotten or forgiven by Kate, he hit Claire again and again with his flat hands while Kate tried to restrain him and he flailed her away, slammed her into a wall, but she came at him again, jumped on his back and pounded his head from some fierce courage and quest for fairness that was freed in her that night, was reborn to her, and that in the months to come would only grow and reclaim its rightful place within her.

———

She told Edward and Barbie in the tree house, and they looked at her with great compassion. Her face was bruised and swollen, and the surgeon's fine work on her cheek had been torn open. Claire had applied an ointment and put in temporary stitches because they couldn't see the surgeon for several days.

"I'm so sorry he did this to you," Claire had whispered to her while working on her face. "I don't think he knows what he's doing or why he's doing it. We probably can't even imagine what he's been through, but the war really messed him up, Kate."

"The war," she'd said. "That's no excuse. The war messed up everybody."

"True. But not as much, or differently. I'm hoping that Dr. Elliott can help him."

She'd looked at Claire and seen the bruises on her face and the hurt and conflict in her eyes. She was horrified by all this. It had occurred to her that in the minds of some, women were the prey animal of the species. It was like a door opening to glimpse something shocking and inexcusable very clearly before the door closed again; something one would prefer not to have glimpsed, but there it was.

After shouting at Kate that he didn't want her there, Thomas never formed another sentence. He shouted and sneered single words and growls, and some mornings he also hugged them both and would not let go, as if hoping to be saved by them. He sat at the table looking at them, and he sat in the stuffed chair in the living room with his eyes shut tight and his hands clamped over his ears.

Claire sat with him and talked to him, telling him that if he wanted to live with them, this was simply not acceptable. No matter what the war had done to him. That the war was in the past and this was the now, the very much everyday now.

"Talk to me, Thomas. Please. Form words around your feelings. Your thoughts. Make the effort. Try it. What are you feeling right now?"

She waited.

"Thomas, I know a doctor who specializes in helping men in your condition. His name is Dr. Elliott and I want you to come with me and see him. Thomas, are you listening?"

But he withdrew ever further. She could tell. Emotionally and physically, back into his chair as far as he could with his eyes shut tight and his hands over his ears. And she let him be.

Another time she told him again about their child dying in her arms, baby William, their little boy dying despite the complete blood transfusion; how in her arms he seemed to want to stretch and reach for her face, and then suddenly he moved no more.

She wept describing this, and she kept asking him, begged him, to tell her why he'd never written back about it, never once. Why? And what happened to him that made him like this? What did happen to him in the war, she wanted to know.

She wiped her eyes and blew her nose and sat up straight. "Unburden yourself, Thomas," she said. "Talk to me. Please say something. Form words, Thomas. *Words*. And the girl, Kate . . . remember what I said the other day. Katie *lives* here. I took her in and now she is part of the three of us. So please leave her alone. Do you hear me? Tell me you understand. Leave Kate alone."

But he never gave any response other than his round-eyed, black-eyed, uncomprehending stare, and soon she came to prefer him when he sat in his corner with his eyes shut tight and his hands clamped over his ears.

He slept on the fold-out couch in the living room, but in the nights they could hear the stairs creaking under his weight, could hear him tiptoeing around and opening doors and drawers and closing them. It was the kitchen drawers that worried Claire, and she took out all the forks and knives and hid them.

She pleaded once more with him to go and see Dr. Elliott, but he would not, and none of her words even seemed to be making contact.

The day after the attack Kate had telephoned Trevor at the mill and said she'd had a little accident and was sorry but she wouldn't be able to come to work for a week or so. He'd lis-tened and said, "All right, Kate. Look after yourself, but come back as soon as you can. Let me know."

In Dr. Shaw's office, too, she referred to it as an accident. Sitting under the bright light, she said she had tripped over something and fallen. She hoped it would also explain the bruises, but it didn't. She could tell from his expression and his tone.

"A fall," he said. "We can't do this too often, you know. It's living tissue, not a shoe."

He asked his nurse to scrub up and to assist him, and then with Kate in the bright light in the surgery chair he worked on the injury in such a masterful way that Claire, who'd asked to be allowed to observe, could only admire him.

"The lines may not be quite as fine this time," he said after-ward. "That's what happens when tissue that's knitted gets ripped apart again. So, no more falls, yes?"

Claire spoke with Dr. Elliott, and he agreed to come to the house. He spent a long time with Thomas in the living room and she listened at the door and could hear mostly the doctor, asking all the right questions of his profession in a caring tone, digging, digging for the deep cause of all this. Then, suddenly, in an explosive change of mood she heard Thomas crying out, not words but screams, and then came slapping and scuf-fling sounds. She opened the door and rushed in to help.

Dr. Elliott was standing and his chair had fallen over. He had a nosebleed and was holding his head back, pinching a nostril. Thomas glared at her, then he turned away and sat down in the corner chair and covered his face with both hands.

In the kitchen Dr. Elliott sat leaning back for a while, holding a handkerchief to his nose.

"I should have seen it coming," he said nasally. "But I didn't. My fault."

She put the kettle on and made a pot of tea and set out condensed milk and sugar.

He took away the handkerchief, sat upright and sniffed. "He's an extreme case, Claire. Absolute shutdown and no signalling. No words, did you notice? It's interesting, that. A form of denial, and instinctual violence from a deep level. I'd say some of that was suppressed character all along, and then something in the war peeled off the social layer. We can try chloral hydrate. If that doesn't work we can try phenobarbital. It's in his eyes, Claire. Can you see it?"

"No. I'm much too close."

"Yes, you are, Claire. And so I am going to tell you what is going on here."

"It's the war, isn't it?"

"To an extent, yes. We see it quite a bit now. Not often so extreme, but we do see it. With Thomas it's more than that. I know your history with him; you yourself let some of it slip early on. A jealous man with a deep anger and a flash temper.

And worse: a violent domination response, and you know what that is. At the moment he's living all kinds of nightmares and he has no idea, and doesn't want to have any idea, of what goes on inside him or around him. Claire, I'm telling you, and you need to hear me when I say that as a result of his closed state and his VDR he is an acute physical danger to you and to Kate."

He rapped a knuckle hard on the table. "Look at me, Claire. Turn this way and let me see your face."

And she blushed and turned to him. She hated and feared this, and felt ashamed, but she held still while he studied her face. In the direct window light he would of course see the bruises under dabs and wipes of facial powder. And he did. She saw it in his eyes.

"Claire, you know of course that as his spouse you will absolutely not be able to help him. For all we know you are contributing to his problems, triggering them in unknown ways, and the same goes for Kate. It's all deep inside his head. You know that, and you also know that as his spouse you are not supposed to—are not *allowed*, even—to medicate him. Yes? By the ethics of our profession. Did you hear me say that as well? Let me prescribe something, and you make sure he takes it. The violence is worrying. In fact he may be beyond the Riverdale. He probably is."

"Meaning?"

"A mental hospital, of course. Scarborough Manor, for instance. At the moment Scarborough is sponsored by a charity and run by Council, at least for as long as their money lasts. They've had success with electroconvulsive therapy. With lithium as well, but lithium would be the last option. So let's wait a bit. I'll prescribe something and we'll see how he responds."

"Thank you, John."

"How is Kate? How is she coming along? Did she tell you that I saw her not that long ago at Riverdale? We had a little talk."

"Yes, she did tell me. How is she? Thomas went after her first. She tried to fight him off and she tried to defend me, but he hurt her and I feel very badly about that."

He looked at her and said nothing, but it was all there in his eyes.

"I thought we could be a family, John."

"A family. Dear Claire, really. You *are* a family. But not all families are happy little picture book families. In fact, in my experience very few are. How is Kate? Is she in?"

"No, she's out on an errand. Her ribs have knitted but it's the injury on her cheek that I'm still worried about. When he hit her it opened up again. We saw Dr. Shaw and he repaired the damage. It's my fault, indirectly, and I know it. I also know that if I had a choice between the two of them, I'd much rather have Kate than him."

"I hope you hear yourself saying all this, Claire. Is she working? She was talking about a job at the mill."

"She did get that job, and she was working there already when this happened. Now she has to take some time off until her cheek is healed again. She's looking for more work to keep her out of the house. She's strong, John. Inside."

"Yes, she is. I know that about her. But don't have her be alone with him if you can help it. If necessary—wait, in a few weeks, when the new physio equipment room is ready, tell her to come and see me. Maybe they can use her there. It'll be up to the matron, of course, but let's hope. It would be good for Kate."

Dr. Elliott wrote out his prescription and signed it. He capped his pen and put it away.

"Lock the bedroom doors, and do not hand him anything. Be careful, Claire, and keep your distance. Dose out the medication and put it on the table, then step back and talk to him."

"I'll do that. Thank you, John."

In the hall they stopped to listen for sounds from the living room. There were none.

Claire and Kate bought two sets of hooks and eyebolts at the hardware store and installed them on the inside of their bedroom doors. If Thomas heard them drilling and whispering he gave no sign. He had not changed, had made no progress. During the days he would sit in his chair and shut down, and at night he would go on the prowl. The piano had been tuned but transport other than a horse and carriage on iron rims had yet to be found, and in the dark he hammered out discordant notes up and down the keyboard. Doors and drawers could again be heard opening and closing, the stairs creaking under his bare feet. Once in a while he knocked on their bedroom doors in the night and scared them bolt-upright in their beds with their hearts pounding. The hook and eye-bolt on Kate's door gave way the first time he pushed hard against it. Kate leapt out of bed screaming and prepared to fend him off, and Claire came running. Next day they installed stronger hooks.

Fifteen

EDWARD'S UNCLE DELBERT came home, and Edward said he hardly recognized him. He'd been a sergeant and a platoon leader in the war, and had been decorated for bravery when he'd rescued two men under fire. Now Delbert, when he came to visit, would sit on the parlour couch, hunched and quiet and his eyes so strange. A different man; years younger than his brother had been, but no longer the robust, kind, and helpful one Edward remembered. His hands trembled, and he spilled his tea and the cup rattled when he set it down.

"I heard about Walter," he said to Edward. "Your dad." He looked down at his hands on the table and moved them closer together. "A good man, he was. Honest and courageous. Let's hope he still had his faith in the end. It would have helped him."

"Helped him with what?"

"With dying, Eddie. Not an easy business, that. There's regular dying and then there's dying in the mud, all ripped apart. Some died clean, but many more did not. Many more. The things

I saw, it makes you want to hide your face and weep. It does. One day in Italy a convent got shelled, a convent full of nuns and novices. I'll never forget that, never. Haunts me, boy. One young novice, she broke my heart, she did . . ."

Delbert stopped and looked down at his hands, looked up at Edward.

"If you ever want me to, I can tell you what it was really like over there. So you know the truth, not the phony bullshit hero gloss on it, but the truth underneath. What the politicians don't want us to know because they want us dumb and eager. But you need to ask me. It's how it works. Especially you, studying to be a pilot now."

"All right."

Over the next few weeks Edward saw his uncle often, but he never asked him about the war. One day when he was walking with Kate, they saw Delbert and they crossed the street and Edward made the introductions. Delbert and Kate talked a bit, and less than a minute into this encounter Edward saw Delbert smile for the first time since he was back. A surprised little smile to begin with, but getting warmer and more open quickly, surely caused by what Delbert saw and felt; by the effect Kate had on him.

—

Edward's mother said Delbert could take whatever clothes he wanted from his dead brother's closet. Walter's closet. He took some socks and sock holders, and two pairs of brogues and shirts and slacks and jackets and suspenders and a good suit. And Edward's mother got out her sewing box and sat in the chair by the window with the light in her lap, and she sewed for days, moving buttons closer in on the jackets and narrowing the waists on trousers.

"There," she said when he'd put the suit. She ran her hands over the shoulders. "Not too bad, Delbert. Very nice, in fact. Looks good on you. Stand up straight. There."

They shared coupons and Delbert came often for dinner, and sometimes he cooked. Sometimes he spent a night on the couch, but never more than one night. The building where he'd had a flat had been destroyed in the bombings, and now he lived at the Elgin Street residence for returned soldiers. He called it the Elgin, like a hotel, and he liked it there, he told them, liked the camaraderie and the lack of pretence. There was a telephone in the office, and the place was inexpensive, clean, and well kept. For him, in his present state, it was like a waiting room at a railroad station, he said. Thinking time. Thinking about the next leg of the journey.

"And listen," he said to Edward. "That girlfriend of yours. With the cheek, what was her name?"

"Kate. She was bombed out. Her father and mother and aunt are dead, and her house is gone. She lives with Dr. Giroux."

"She's nice, Eddie. Special. Look after that. After what you've got with her."

When Delbert heard about Kate's situation with Thomas, he told Edward he'd be willing to teach her self-defence and about weapons of convenience, as he called them. How to spot them instantly in a room, and then how to use them. A chair, a lamp, a book, a vase, a pencil; in the right hands almost any object could be used as a weapon.

"Just watch out for her face," said Edward. "Nothing, absolutely nothing, should touch that cheek."

"I know that," said Delbert.

At first Barbie wanted to be taught as well, but she dropped out soon because she became worried about her hands. From then on she sat on the piano stool in the church basement and watched as Delbert, Kate, and Edward simulated kicks and turns and blows in slow motion, using imaginary objects found in imaginary rooms.

One day Delbert brought a tall, heavy walking cane, and he held it up and said, "Today I'm going to show you how to swing a stick. Good weapon, that, and almost any stick will do, as long as it's solid and the right length. Watch me swing it."

He swung the stick in slow motion. "Legs, hips, arms, and shoulders," he said. "See that? Step into it for momentum and swing with your whole body. Your turn, Kate. Show me."

She did, and Delbert watched closely.

"Not bad," he said. "Do it again. Arms, shoulders, hips, everything."

"You'd need space to swing a stick like that," said Kate. "It wouldn't work in a bedroom."

"In a small space you can hold it shorter, or poke it, hard. That's good too. But in a bedroom there's other weapons. The bedside lamp for hitting. The lamp cord for strangling. A chair. Hold it legs-forward and run at him hard. The main thing is, never hesitate. Pin him to the wall and then kick him, you know where. Swing the stick again, Kate. Then we'll do the chair over there."

One day, at the end of a session, Delbert told Kate that there was something else he was thinking of for her. He looked at his watch. "It's too late now, but meet me tomorrow at the back of my building. It's at 48 Elgin. At ten o'clock. Can you do that?"

"Yes, I can. I'm not working at the mill right now."

"Good. At ten, then. And keep the bandage on your cheek."

"Oh, I will. At least until the stitches are out, and maybe a bit longer. What's this about?"

"You'll see. I'm developing a little sideline, and if you could help out with a few errands there'd be good money in it for you. Real good. I'll show you tomorrow."

———

At five to ten the next morning she stood waiting among the bushes at the back of his building. He came out, carrying a closed canvas market bag, and he set it down by her feet. He looked at her from head to toe, then he handed her four one-pound notes and a piece of paper with an address on it.

"It's in East London," he said. "Down by the docks. I want you to take a taxi and go there with this bag. There are many bomb sites and damaged roads. The taxi can't go all the way but it'll get you close. Walk down a few dirt lanes towards a place called Terrace Warehouse. It's written on it in big letters, high up. Just find your way to it, and then on the river side of it go to the back of this address. There's a grey iron door at ground level with the number ten on it in black paint. Knock on it, two good hard knocks. A man called Denver is waiting there for you, and he'll give you one hundred pounds for the bag. Please repeat that for me. What are you going to do?"

And she repeated it. Down by the docks go to the river side of Terrace Warehouse, find this address, at the back there's a grey iron door with a black number ten on it, two hard knocks. Denver, collect one hundred pounds.

"Good," he said. "Then get back in a taxi and come here. Use the front entrance and just ask for me. You'll give me ninety pounds, the rest is yours."

"Ten pounds? I get to keep *ten pounds*?" She couldn't work it out so quickly, but it would take many weeks to earn that much at her mill job.

"Yes. I don't think you'll need more than four pounds for taxis, but if you do, take it from the hundred. Okay? Don't drop the bag. Hold it like you've just been to the market or something. Don't make eye contact with anybody. Be aware of what goes on around you, but pay no real attention to it. Just keep walking, calm and straight and upright like you do anyway. There's an injury on your face but you're not letting it get to you. Deliver the bag and come back."

"What's in the bag?"

He shook his head. "Best if you don't know. Can you do it?"

She picked up the bag, slung the handles over her right shoulder and kept the bag close to her side under her arm. It was not very heavy.

"All right?" he said.

Sixteen

AS SOON AS THE STITCHES were out she went back to her job at the mill.

"What happened?" said Trevor.

"I re-injured my cheek. But it's all better now."

She lifted the bandage to show him and he nodded and said, "Good."

The legs and arms on her boiler suit were still rolled up to the right length, and she put the suit on and went to work. She liked this job. Liked being able to do it and being part of something again.

That day she and Trevor took a fresh-air break together, out on the millrun bridge. There had been a lot of rain that spring and even now, in June, the river was still high and brown and it carried branches and newspapers and garbage. The raker told them that some days entire bushes and even trees came floating down from the flood lands.

And worse.

One day on her shift the body of a young woman perhaps her own age in a green coat and a pleated tartan skirt was caught in the grate. She and Trevor and the raker used log tongs to pull the woman up onto the walkway planks. Fist-size stones were weighing down her coat pockets, and the three of them stood silenced and in awe as the young woman lay there with her small hands by her side, and her eyes wide open.

Kate told Edward and Barbie about it in the tree house, and she told Claire. Claire had already heard, and she knew that the medical examiner had ruled it a suicide. The stones had been a clue, of course; in addition, river water had been found in the woman's lungs, and there'd been no injuries other than the post-mortem marks that would have been caused by the log tongs.

"She was pregnant," said Claire. "About four months, the ME said."

In order to identify the woman, the police released an artist's sketch of her, as she might have looked in life. Kate pinned a copy of it to a wall in the tree house, to remember her like this, not the way she'd looked lying on the planks.

She called her Moira, and when she was alone in the tree house, waiting for the other two, or just for Edward, Moira was her silent companion. Together they looked out onto the trees and flowers and birds and the stone angel in the changing light, and the busy life around the flooded bomb crater, water lilies now and frogs and ducks.

All her savings had been in her handbag, lost during the bombing. So had the business card of the lawyer where she and her mother had signed papers, and the keys on the little ribbon David had given her. She thought that surely the handbag couldn't be very far from where she herself had been found, and she decided to look for it. It was early summer by now; the hoarding had been up for months and maybe a panel in it had come loose, or maybe she could pry away one of the panels and get in that way.

Edward said he'd help, and next afternoon they went there, with her riding on the luggage carrier of his bicycle. He'd brought a torch and a pry bar, which he used on a joint in the panels at the back of the bomb site. Minutes later they were in.

She knew exactly where to look, where the walkout from the basement room had been. Where the table and couch would have stood, and where the neighbours and the wardens and the dog had dug down already to find her. What she did not know was what the force of the blast would have done to her handbag.

They worked until near dark, shifting lumber and bricks and concrete, peering into spaces, and just when they were about to give up they found the handbag. It was under the couch. The couch was flattened and its legs were broken, and only a short end of the torn strap showed in the beam of Edward's torch. He used a piece of wood for a fulcrum under his pry bar and with it was able to raise the couch high enough to ease out the handbag, one careful, wiggling tug at a time.

Then he crawled out backwards.

"My hero," she said when they were clear of the rubble. She gave him a hug and a kiss, and he held her and put his face against her good cheek. They secured the gap in the hoarding and bicycled home through the evening like successful treasure hunters.

"What is it you're doing for Delbert?" asked Edward along the way. She sat with her arms around his waist and her feet on the little footrests that he'd fixed to the axle bolts.

"Deliveries. A bag with stuff. I've done a few now, for ten pounds each. Can you believe it? Ten pounds!"

"What stuff?"

"I don't know. And I don't care. He pays for the taxis, too. And he wants me to wear a bandage."

"Why? And you don't know what's in the bags? What's it feel like? Hard, soft, heavy?"

"Hard and clunky. Not too heavy. But don't pry, Eddie. You said you trusted him. I do too."

When she came home, the house was in darkness. Claire was on night shift, and in the living room where Thomas spent most of his time all was quiet. She tiptoed up the stairs to her room and emptied the handbag onto the desk. There were the keys to her house that was gone, a broken slice of very dry bread, a handkerchief with her initials, the lawyer's business card, David's secret keys tied together with the ribbon, and all her savings in a red leather purse. It was money she'd put aside over time, sixpence an hour, and it had added up. She counted it: forty-four pounds and nine shillings. Added to the mill money and the Delbert money now, she had more than one hundred pounds. A fortune.

She sat on the chair and picked up bits of bread and nibbled on them in celebration, letting the crumbs soak in her mouth. Stale bread, but bread with a history from home.

In the morning she tried David's keys, just to make sure they still worked before she returned the keys Tony had given her. For a while she stood unmoving in the secret room. It seemed to her that there was a slightly wider space between two of the short floorboards in the corner, as if one board had been shifted. She knelt, inserted the letter opener, and pried up two boards and lifted them off. The manuscript was still there, tied up as before. But was it? She took it out and looked at the knot more closely. A shoelace knot. Was that what she'd used? Not a square knot? She opened it and then retied it, making both ears exactly the same length.

That day she splurged. For herself she bought a nice second-hand dress with little buttons down the front, a pleated skirt, and a used pair of American blue jeans. She bought two blouses, a matching sweater, and a good Navy outdoor jacket with large black buttons for colder weather. And she bought a used pair of shoes that she loved, to go with the dress, and a pair of nearly new ankle boots that were suitable for both riding and walking.

For Edward she bought a Swiss Army pocket knife, and for Barbie a little silver-and-turquoise necklace. And for Claire she found a soft off-white cotton blouse with a French collar in very good condition that Mr. Bennington at the thrift shop said Claire would absolutely love.

And for Jimmy, the boy who'd alerted the neighbours and saved her life, she bought a blue bicycle. Just the right size for an eight-year-old, Mr. Bennington said. She took it to Jimmy's house in a taxi, and then she and Jimmy's mother watched him climb on it and race up and down the street, grinning from ear to ear.

"Boys," said his mother, and sighed. "We shouldn't reward him for going onto a bomb site, but in this case . . . and look at him."

After all that extravagance she still had seventy-two pounds, one shilling, and sixpence left. She took most of it to the bank and opened an account; the rest she planned to keep in her purse once the cobbler on Trinity Lane had mended the strap on the handbag.

She went back to the bomb site a few more times, sometimes with Edward, sometimes alone. When she was there with him, she sat close to him to feel his warmth. One night she brought a blanket and they lay down.

"You can touch me, Eddie," she said.

He stroked her face, even on the scarred side, and he kissed her closed eyes. He was undoing the buttons on her dress when she put her hand on his and whispered, "No, Eddie, not just yet." Her voice trembled a bit when she said it, and he kissed her skin where he'd opened the dress and then he did the buttons up again. She felt sorry immediately and the next time on the blanket in the nighttime rubble, she let him make love to her because she wanted it as badly as he. Afterward he held her for a long time.

Seventeen

THE SURGEON'S REPAIR had not been able to bring back his original fine line, but the scar wasn't too bad. It looked a bit like a check mark, and it still pulled at the left corner of her mouth like a constant crooked smile. But she was getting used to it and most of the time she no longer wore a bandage.

One night at their sit-down she said, "Claire, there's something I want to ask you. It's about . . . it's just that Edward and I . . ."

She stopped, feeling self-conscious about it suddenly.

"What?" said Claire.

"You must be tired. We can talk some other time."

"No, what is it?" Claire's expression changed. "Oh, oh. Why do I think I know? *Edward and I*, you started to say. Kate, look at me and tell me that you are taking precautions."

"I know about counting the days."

"That's one way. Tomorrow I'll bring you something much better. Put it in right, and it's about ninety per cent safe. There'll be detailed instructions with it. Make sure you follow them."

She did more deliveries for Delbert. The bags were getting heavier and he was paying her twelve pounds now, sometimes thirteen. One time when he sent her off on a run with a heavy bag, Delbert told her that this time she would be collecting three hundred thirty pounds. He said to be sure and count the money.

"That much," she said, shocked.

"Yes, but don't think about it. Just act like you always do. Imagine you're going home from the market. Maybe you've got groceries in there, vegetables or something. Keep calm inside. Whatever is on the inside shows on the outside. You know that."

He stood looking at her. Not unkindly, never that, but taking his time to see her clearly: no bandage covering the scar on her cheek anymore, the yellowed bruises on her face. The burnt areas in her hair filled in now, a bit more coarse, but chestnut-gold like the rest.

"All right, Kate?"

She nodded.

"Good. This time you get to keep twenty. Same target address. I'll be here, waiting."

———

In the back seat of the taxi she put her hand inside the bag: hard-edged things wrapped in newspaper. She took one out and unwrapped it in the light from the side window. It was a large pistol. The writing on the side said *Browning*. She looked into the bag and counted five more. She wrapped the Browning again, tucked them all in, and wished she hadn't looked.

At the same spot as always she paid the driver and continued on foot, a winding back route to the grey iron door where the taxi could not go. Dirt lanes with grit in the air. Bomb sites and shattered bricks everywhere. Many of the hoardings pulled down and taken away, probably for firewood. Men in groups of three and four loitering, leaning against walls, watching her. And this time, surely because she knew what was in the bag, she felt self-conscious. She made nervous eye contact, felt afraid and tried not to show it. She could hear a ship's horn, could hear loading cranes rattling beyond the warehouses to her left. And all the men watching her. One of them called out, "Need any help with that bag, luv? What you got there?"

He pushed himself off the broken wall he'd been leaning against and came her way. A torn cap on his head, narrowed eyes. A dirty hand reaching out. She almost froze for fear he might grab her or grab the bag, but for some reason he didn't. He stood and looked at her, then he lowered his hand and just watched her go by. He said something to the others over his shoulder and one of them chuckled, but they left her alone. At the end of the lane she turned the corner and then another, and finally there was the building with the grey iron door.

She told Edward and Claire, and they were both angry at Delbert for letting her take such risks. Edward said he'd talk to him, and Claire said that no amount of money was worth that risk; a twofold risk because the guns were certainly illegal, and asking her to carry them through back lanes in that difficult part of town—what was he thinking?

She went to see Delbert, and he listened to her and thought about it. Then he said that Edward and Claire had a point, but they were exaggerating the danger. It was true that there was crime in the East End, but probably not much more than any-where else. Petty crime mostly, caused by poverty, which was caused in turn by a lack of work and opportunity. So much industry destroyed there in the bombings.

"But you decide," he said. "And you shouldn't have looked. I meant it when I said it was best not to know. Fear changes how we come across. And the bandage helped too. It made you look injured but brave. The money is good, Kate, isn't it? And there's more, and great demand at the moment. It's guns that the men brought home from the war. British revolvers and German, Italian, and American pistols. Russian Makarovs, even. And the prices are going up."

He paused and shook his head.

"Kate, this isn't some kind of career. It's just a good short-term opportunity to build some capital. It won't last. I'm going to make the most of it, and I want to include you in it."

"And I am grateful," she said. "But can I ask why you're not taking them there yourself, rather than pay me?"

"For one thing because I'm doing very well with my profit, and for the other because I like you and I know your story. I want to help you earn some money while this opportunity lasts. And then it's also because there's something about you that I don't have and it works very well for you. It's all in the how, Kate. In how you move and look and hold your head. It's in your eyes. And because of the way you came across until now it was highly unlikely that anyone would stop you. So don't think about what's in the bag. Just look like you know where you're going and keep walking. Maybe put the bandage back on and take the taxi a bit further and then loop back. You know the building, you know the iron door."

She said she'd think about it and let him know.

In the meantime, because there was surely more under all the rubble at the bomb site that could be salvaged, she spoke to the lawyer and he wrote out a legal declaration of her status. With that document she made inquiries at town hall about a cleanup, and they said that in general and for the time being there was no help available with private property. However, in this case, since schools had opened up again and the location was close to a school and posed a dangerous temptation for boys, an exception could be made. The town would clear the lot and dispose of the rubble in a landfill site, and anything still useable would be set aside.

One day not long after that, she saw them do it. A steam shovel scooping up bricks and bits of burnt and broken lumber with its enormous jaws and dumping them on lorries; pieces of what had been furniture and shreds of clothing and of lives now gone. Two men stood near the steam shovel, watching.

There were few items that were still useable, most of them from the front cellar. Among them were her bicycle, a chair, a few pots and pans, and her mother's black suitcase, however dented and burnt at one corner.

While the steam shovel kept working, the two men pried open the suitcase and went through the contents. Kate saw them do that, and she stepped into the gap in the hoarding and called to them over the noise of the steam shovel.

"Hello! Who are you? And what are you doing?"

She moved closer.

"Stay where you are!" called one of them. "We're just making sure it's all safe."

She recognized him. He was the one who'd brought her the sunflower picture.

"Of course it's safe! It's my mother's old suitcase!"

"Well, just checking. Don't come any closer."

"All right, but bring it over here when you're done. And bring my bicycle."

It was a good ladies' bike with a Sturmey-Archer gear hub and a full chain guard. She was glad to see it. It was bent in places and one wheel had lost most of its spokes, but later that day Edward said he could fix all that. He'd find a new wheel, and there were tools and machinery at the RCAF base that could straighten things much stiffer than a bicycle frame.

When Edward brought the bike back in good working order she tried it at first for short rides around town, and then for longer ones. The mill work and exercising with the sandbag had strengthened her, and the pain in her ribs was mostly gone. Her breathing was much better as well, and on a day when she hadn't had to fend off Thomas in a while and the bruises on her face were hardly noticeable, she rode her bike out to the horse farm.

When she came around the final turn she did not ring the bicycle bell as usual, but the horses saw or sensed her anyway, and the near ones stood with their heads up and Princess came trotting to the gate.

Kate used the door knocker at the main building, and only when no one came to the door did she mount her bike again and ride down to the barn.

Mrs. Fitzhenry was there, in the half dark in the back. She was nailing a label onto a stall, and when she saw Kate in the open barn door she stood the hammer on the ground and came up.

"Yes," she said. "Kate. What is it?"

"I'm all better now, Mrs. Fitzhenry. And I could come and work here again. Feeding and exercising Princess. I'd like to. Could I please?"

"I heard about your misfortune. A woman came and told us."

"That was Dr. Giroux. She's become a good friend and support."

"Has she now. But you see, when we didn't hear from you and we needed help we hired someone else. The McMurtry girl. Anne. Do you know her?"

"Yes, I do, Mrs. Fitzhenry. I didn't know she could ride."

"She can, more or less, and with practice she'll get better. It wouldn't be fair to let her go again so soon. She's done nothing wrong. And she's reliable, Kate."

"I am reliable too. It's just that after the bomb I was in hospital and I couldn't let you know sooner. I had injuries."

"I'm sure. And I'm sorry that there's nothing for you here right now. I can't really . . . no, I'm happy with Anne."

"Could I at least come and ride Princess? We're good together, and you wouldn't have to pay me."

"To ride Princess? You should be paying me for that pleasure. Come on, Kate. You know that's not how it works."

Mrs. Fitzhenry stood and watched her.

"All right, Kate? Off you go. And when you leave here, just leave. Do not talk to Princess and do not walk up to her."

"I can't even go and say hello? I brought her a little apple."

"No, Kate. Let me see you get on your bike and pedal off."

She stood looking at this hard woman. "But she's at the gate waiting for me. It would mean a lot to me if I could just—"

"No! You heard me. Let's not confuse the horse. Off you go, girl. If there is a change I'll find you and I'll let you know."

She not only missed the horses, she also needed to be busier, needed to keep out of Thomas's way at the house, and she wanted to earn more money. And so she did as Delbert had suggested and plotted three different routes to the target address. Then, all summer long and well into fall, she did many more runs for him; as many as he would give her. For the runs she taped a bandage back on and put bunches of carrots or beets from her garden into the bag and let the green tops hang out. And she walked briskly away from the taxi, alternating her route along other back lanes and past other bomb sites and lurking men, turning corners and watching her step, and soon there was the building and the iron door. She gave it two hard knocks and stood back, waiting for Denver.

Eighteen

SHE WROTE about it all on the Underwood in David's room, pages of notes to work through it all. She felt badly about keeping the room a secret from Claire and Edward, but it was something she'd promised to do, and her solitude in it and sitting at David's typewriter and typing notes to him and to herself became something she looked forward to.

Dear David,

My cheek is better and I'm keeping busy, earning money at the mill and for doing deliveries for Edward's uncle Delbert. I often look at the photographs in Mum's little black suitcase that I rescued from the house. The four of you in Oxford. I wish you were here to explain them to me. Picnics, and all of you in swimming costumes by some lake. Mum looked so pretty.

So much is happening. I love Edward, always did, ever since we met in the tree house and started seeing each other, and he says he loves me too. I can feel that. Perhaps one day I'll marry him. I can talk to Claire about it all. I don't understand her with Thomas, dangerous as he is, but since in all other things she is always clear and right, I am willing to give the situation time. With Thomas she makes me think of that line from Turgenev you gave me once, that another's heart is a dark forest.

And you? Where are you? You said to burn all your papers if you ever disappeared, but I can't do it because I'm still hoping you'll be back. That is one door I cannot close, at least not yet, and I hope I'll never have to.

Missing you,

Kate

One day at their meeting spot behind the Elgin, Delbert showed her an unusual pistol that had come his way. "It's a Beretta pocket pistol," he said. "A souvenir that someone took from a dead Italian. It's rare because they were issued only to a small number of senior officers. It's much more compact than their regular side piece, but it fires the same nine-millimetre round. They're in great demand, these guns. Watch."

His hands moved and in seconds he had the gun stripped into four pieces: magazine, barrel, slide, and grip. He let her look through the barrel.

"Clean as a whistle," he said. "No nicks, no scratches." He reassembled the gun and handed it to her. "Hold it and point it at the ground."

She took it and he adjusted her grip, two-handed, with the butt of the gun resting in the palm of her left hand.

"Cross your thumbs, left over right. Gives you more control. Maybe one day soon Edward can book us a session at the Canadian range. Give you an opportunity to shoot a handgun."

She handed it back. "Why are you showing it to me?"

"Because it would be a very good investment for you. Do me three twenty-pound runs at no charge and it's yours. Keep it for a while and you'll make a very nice profit with it. Guaranteed."

"It's illegal, isn't it?"

"Yes, of course it is. Half the good stuff being sold now is illegal. The black market, Kate, in difficult times. But I want to help you put aside some money for when you need it. That's what I'm doing. Stash some money while I can. The present conditions won't last, and this gun is a collector's item already."

"I'd have to think about where to hide it," she said. "Can't keep it at home because of Thomas. No, wait . . . I think I know a good spot."

Edward was at first reluctant, but then he did apply for and receive permission to bring them to the Canadian firing range as his guests; they drove there in a car that Delbert borrowed from a friend. The range consisted of the warden's hut and seven stations with loading benches and railroad-tie backstops in an abandoned gravel pit outside of town. It was the end of July and the day was hot and humid, and when they arrived there they were the only shooters. The range warden had them read the safety rules, sign that they had done so, and then sign in with their full names, dates of birth, and addresses.

"You be careful now," he said to them. "The moment I see a barrel pointing anywhere other than down-range, you're gone. And pick up your shells." He looked at Kate. "You ever shot a handgun, lady?"

"No. But I've got two good instructors here and I'll be very careful."

"You'd better be," said the warden. "Like I said: point down-range, always. Always. Down-range, even when the gun is empty."

Edward was unhappy the entire time.

"I know I agreed," he said to her. "But I still don't understand why you want to do this."

But Delbert was on her side. "Why wouldn't she, Eddie? She's learning something new. Leave her be. It's kind of special and a good skill to have. We never know when we might need it. There are no other shooters here today to distract her, so let her practise. She's not doing badly, got two in the black already. It'll be your turn next."

"I just don't want her to *buy* a gun. Own one. To begin with, it's a burden. And it's dangerous. Too many people get shot with their own handguns."

"Not so loud, Eddie," said Kate. "We don't want the warden to think we're having an argument. And it's all right. I'm enjoying this."

That day she learned how to load and unload a handgun, and how to take one apart, clean it, and reassemble it: barrel, slide, grip, and magazine. She learned the right stance, with her left leg a bit forward and the knee loose, and she learned the right grip for a handgun, one-fisted and two-fisted, and how to concentrate on the front sight in the target. And she learned to let recoil happen and then to bring the gun down again for the next shot.

She soon realized that she was actually quite good at this, and from then on she was no longer nervous at all. She was learning a skill that she hoped she would never need, but it was interesting, and just in case she ever did, this was the opportunity to learn it.

"Centre mass," Delbert kept saying to her in front of the man-target. "Don't bother too much with aiming. No time for that. He'll be quite close anyway, so just point at the biggest part of him and pull the trigger twice. Bam, bam."

Later in the car Edward said to her, "So you're really buying it? Where are you going to keep it?"

"In a safe place."

"Where? You're not taking it home, are you? Not with Thomas poking around."

"Eddie, can you please just trust me with this? It's an investment—right, Delbert?"

"It certainly is. And a good one. Much better than stocks or bonds."

At that moment she wondered for the first time if perhaps the time had come to tell Edward and Claire about the secret room. No, not Edward yet, she decided without knowing why. But Claire, maybe.

Nineteen

AT HOME THOMAS WAS SHOWING no improvement. He refused the food they served him and helped himself to leftovers in the icebox. And he refused to drink from the glasses Claire set out for him; chloral hydrate and phenobarbital, according to Dr. Elliott's prescription. He took neither; he poured the liquids out on the table, and when Claire wiped up he would try to snatch her hand. The one time she tried to insist that he drink, he threw the glass at her. It struck her on the forehead and caused a laceration that needed three stitches. Kate, too, had new bruises on her face. The surgeon's repair held, but from one of the blows her good cheek developed a bulging haematoma that Claire had to drain with a syringe.

"Can you please explain to me why you are so patient with him?" Kate said to Claire that night in the kitchen. "Why put up with all this? The man is a dangerous mental case. What are you still hoping for?"

"For a sign of recovery, Kate. I know how weak this must sound, but we don't know what he's been through, and some of them do recover. I've seen it. He's also my husband, and there was a time when I did love him."

"He must have been very different then. Shhh . . . listen."

"What?"

The wall clock ticked loudly. Three thirty in the morning. Through the pebbled-glass portion of the kitchen door, they could see that the light in the hall had come on. A shadow moving out there.

They did not stir. Kate with her index finger across her lips. She took it away.

"I think he's going up to the bathroom," she whispered. "Why? When he could use the one down here. And look at us. Like scared little rabbits in your own home. It's not good, Claire."

"I know it's not." Claire stood up and strode to the door and opened it wide. Thomas stood there in his rumpled pyjamas, blinking in the light like a sleepy boy.

"Is everything all right, Thomas?"

He said nothing. Just stood there a moment longer, then he turned towards the stairway. Claire closed the door and sat down again.

After a while she said, "It's hard to explain, Kate. Maybe even impossible. But he was different then. I was too, and I ignored certain signs. Saw them and ignored them, hoping they would go away. Seeing and feeling what I wished to see and feel. In retrospect, my love for him might have been mostly the fact that I wanted—or as a biologist might say, that my body wanted—children. Then he changed and I changed, too . . . and now the war, and what it may have done to him."

"You could just leave him, Claire. Divorce him for battery and abuse."

"Legally I probably could."

"So?"

"I'd feel guilty. Emotionally I still feel trapped in the spaces between my roles as a wife and a physician and the person I want to be. I feel I should see it through a while longer."

"What's a while, Claire?"

"Katie, please. Just a short while longer? For my sake, not his."

Kate sat looking at her. She looked away and toyed with the handle of her teacup.

"Can we, please?" said Claire.

Kate looked up and raised a finger. Thomas was coming down the stairs and the light in the hallway went off, then on again. They both sat unmoving, looking at the distorted image in the pebbled glass with no idea of what might happen next. Then the light went out and they heard the living room door open and close.

———

Next day, when she came home from work, Claire confronted Thomas once again. He was still in his pyjamas, sitting in a chair at the table, watching her.

"Thomas," she said. "We can't go on like this. You've been home more than two months now without any improvement. You need help. I was hoping that I could give it to you, but I am beginning to see that I cannot. I can't give you the help you need, Thomas. So, I will be speaking with Dr. Elliott and I'm hoping he'll come once more to try and help you. And this time you'll have to do what he says. You may have to go into a hospital. Do you understand?"

She waited for him to say something, anything that showed he was following her.

"What happened to you in the war, Thomas? If you don't want to tell me, tell Dr. Elliott. It would help you to talk about it."

He sat staring at her. His deep-set eyes round and black. His lips moving soundlessly.

"Thomas?"

His strong hands forming fists on the table and flattening out. Flexing and relaxing. She could remember her fascination with those hands, and sitting here now could even remember the thrill of the entire thing. So strange. The same old blundering into an adventure that she thought she'd be able to control, and as a loving wife and medical doctor could learn from and grow with.

And sitting across the table now, years later but not all that many years, he smiled at her, or tried to smile, but it was just a horror mask that she could no longer bear to look at.

"Please say something, Thomas."

But he did not. He raised his hands and covered his face.

That night around two in the morning, Thomas with all his weight behind him broke the strong hook and eyebolt on Kate's door. He burst into her room and grabbed her ankle and dragged her out of bed with her shoulders and head bouncing on the floor. She fought back and was able to twist and kick herself free and she stood up, grabbed the lamp on the bedside table, and in a fierce entire-upper-body swing smashed it base-first against the side of his head.

He stared at her in wide-eyed astonishment, brought a hand up to his temple, and fell down.

By then Claire had come running and she turned on the overhead light and saw what had happened. She helped him up and in the bathroom rinsed the blood from his face and dried it and then put him to bed on the couch. Through the closed door Kate could hear Claire weeping. Could hear her whispering to herself, or to him. She loved Claire and would always love her and would always be grateful, but this—*what was this?* She leaned into the panel with her ear pressed to the wood and knew only that the sounds and the emotions touched her deeply, even if she could not understand them.

They met in the kitchen and neither she nor Claire said anything for a long time. They sat on the chairs in the dimly lit room with the wall clock ticking and the first silver showing at the rim of their world beyond the trees and the Talbot River. Claire still had Thomas's blood on the sleeve of her nightgown.

Finally Kate took the lead.

"I had no choice, Claire. He yanked me out of bed and—"

Claire raised a hand to stop her. For a moment they sat in silence, then Kate said, "Would it be better if I moved out? Wouldn't it make all this easier for you? I have some money now, and I can earn more and rent a place of my own. You and I would still be the very good friends we are now, but I'd be out of your way with Thomas. You could wait him out without having to worry about me."

In the silence the clock ticked loudly. One second . . . two seconds . . . three . . . four . . . She leaned forward and said, "Claire? I think that maybe I should move out."

And Claire stood up, stood for a moment, and then with a stifled cry as from a sudden pain or panic, or perhaps driven away by words she did not wish to hear, she fled across the room to the corner where the tea towels hung, and she stood for a long moment facing the wall.

Finally she turned around, pale and exhausted. "Kate, I know I should have done something sooner. I do know that now. I do."

She came back and sat down.

"I don't . . ." She covered her face with her hands and sat for a moment, then lowered her hands to her lap and said, "I don't want you moving out, Kate. Please. I love having you here, and I need you."

"But look at what's going on."

"I know. I know." Claire reached and put her hand briefly on Kate's hand on the table. "Just a few more days before you decide anything. Just a few more days?"

In the morning they sat in Dr. Elliott's office at Riverdale. Claire told him what had happened and she asked him to come back to the house once more, for a formal psychiatric evaluation of Thomas.

Dr. Elliott listened and he saw Claire's forehead and he agreed. He said he had tried to get Thomas's medical discharge report from the military but apparently it could not be located.

"It was probably destroyed," he said. "Which is often done so as not to give them a burdensome history. In that sense it's bad news."

He took a sheet of paper and made notes. It was very still in the room.

He looked up and said, "Claire, would you mind waiting outside for a minute or two while I have a word with Kate?"

In the waiting room four men and three women sat on chairs along the walls, and they all avoided looking at one another and at her. She knew those sagging shoulders well, those sad faces and inward-looking eyes so dark and still. The fear in them. Because in one way or another it was all about fear. Always, all kinds of fear. Fear being the primary emotion. Not love, but fear. That had been among the first lessons to be grasped in Dr. Elliott's class. The four words written in chalk on the blackboard: NOT LOVE, BUT FEAR. The thing that no one wants to accept, he'd said. Love cannot flourish where there is fear. And so to find love, we must first examine and then conquer fear. And there was a never-ending list of things to be feared. He named a few and could have gone on, he said: fear of rejection, of being shamed, of ridicule, of being found out, of change, of abandonment, of illness, of failure, of old age, of darkness, of bodily harm, and on and on. Fear, often masquerading as something else, often even as courage, was the driver.

"Find it and hold it up to the light, and you're halfway there," he told the class. "The same goes for ourselves, by the way. For the doctor the same as for the patient. By varying degrees, it goes for all of us who still have a heartbeat."

And a multitude of hands had shot up to ask questions.

Dr. Elliott came to the house again and spent another full session with Thomas. Standing in the hall, Claire could hear them through the living room door. The doctor's kind and caring tone, his insistent questions, again and again. Questions that had to be asked and absolutely needed to be answered because therein lay the cure. But Thomas was not responding. He shouted noises, not words, and at some point he must have thrown something because she could hear something hard clattering over the floor.

And so once more she and Dr. Elliott sat in the kitchen while the doctor wrote down his medical opinion and then filled out the commitment form for the mental institution of Scarborough Manor.

He looked up and said, "They'll assess him, Claire. And then they'll decide whether or not to try electroconvulsive therapy. It'll be exclusively up to the doctors there, but I know for a fact that they've had some good results with it. Everything in the body is electrical, with microcurrents everywhere. Nobody knows exactly how ECT works, but it seems that in the right dosage it can have a kind of cleansing effect. It can flush circuits, reset the brain and delete problem memories, and raise the threshold to problem impulses."

He waited for a long moment. Then he said, "Claire. *Dr. Giroux* . . . since his case is a serious psychopathology, and since there is a chance that Scarborough can actually help him, shall we try that route?"

He sat looking at her, waiting. Finally he rapped a knuckle twice on the table.

"Claire? I need to hear you say that you agree or disagree. Which is it?"

And she took a deep breath and let it out, and said, "Yes, I agree. Thank you, John."

Dr. Elliott made the call from the telephone in the hall and he was still there when three men from the institution came to pick Thomas up. He struggled and cried and flung his arms about, and when he struck one of the attendants in the face it took all three to tie his wrists behind his back.

Dr. Elliott and Claire signed the release form, and then the men walked him down the front steps to their car. One of them was carrying the little suitcase she'd packed for Thomas, with a change of clothes and his shaving gear. Under his coat he was still in his pyjamas and his slippers.

Watching, she felt only a small twinge of guilt; mostly she felt relief.

Twenty

ON HER WAY HOME from the interview with the matron at Riverdale, Kate made a quick detour to the tea room. She stood leaning her bicycle against the wall when she heard a man say, "Kate! Is that you?"

It took her a moment to recognize him. He was Patrick Bailey, David's friend from Oxford. This time he was not in uniform; he wore casual slacks and a summer jacket over an open shirt. He said, "Is David here too?"

"David? Don't you know?"

"Know what?"

"David is missing ever since the day he met you here."

"Missing? What do you mean?"

"Just that. Missing on a foreign assignment."

"But . . . how? Kate, please come inside and sit with me for a minute. Talk to me."

They sat by the window and ordered tea. She told him about the men who took David away in the night. "Two men in long coats and hats," she said. "A nightmare image for me, going back to the day my dad was killed. And two months after they'd taken David away we got a letter from the government telling us he'd gone missing, but they would keep us informed. They never did."

She paused for a moment, then she said, "And it gets worse. Not long after that, a bomb fell on our house."

He stared at her. "I had no idea about that either. That late in the war. And you were injured." He touched the side of his face.

"Yes, I was. But my mother and my aunt were killed."

"Oh no! Mary—how terrible." He looked genuinely shocked and saddened. "That's just . . . I'm so sorry to hear it, Kate."

"You didn't know? Really? How could you not, when you were such good friends?"

He looked at her, astonished. He sat back as if he had to think about this.

"What is it, Kate? What am I picking up here? Are you . . . what is it?"

"It's the fact that David disappeared the very night after he met you here. That same night. And when I left the two of you, he looked very unhappy. As though he knew what was coming and you had brought it." She could hear her voice getting hard and loud, and she paused for a moment. "Sorry. But I've been thinking about it ever since."

He sat forward. "Kate," he said earnestly. "How do I . . . David and I simply met for coffee for old times' sake, and because

I was in London. There was nothing sinister about our meeting and I had nothing whatsoever to do with his disappearance. Please believe me."

She sat studying his face, his eyes.

"What is it?" he said. "You are making assumptions and you're choosing to assume the worst. Why not start all over and assume that our meeting that day was simply the friendly get-together that I say it was?"

She took a sip of tea, set the cup down in its saucer, and looked at him. "Was it?"

"Yes, it was. Do you have any idea where he could have gone?"

She nodded. "My mother heard the words *Toronto* and *Reykjavik*. That's all we ever knew. Like a rumour. I called the number in the letter many times and left a message. There were always different people on the telephone. Men and women. Like someone just passing a desk and picking up a phone that happens to be ringing. I never heard back."

"Didn't you? So let me see what I can find out. I do know a few people here and there. How can I get in touch with you?"

She hesitated. Then she said, "I live with a friend. I don't want to give out her phone number, but you can leave a message with the proprietor here. His name is Tony. I'm here quite often. What did David and you talk about, after I left?"

"He told me about a writing project he was working on. He had some questions and I was able to help him a bit. Did he ever say anything to you about that? I mean his project."

She shook her head.

"He kept an office at the house, didn't he?"

"Not really what I'd call an office. A few file boxes."

"File boxes. Was anything salvaged from that? Papers, some kind of manuscript?"

This was suddenly all very strange again, a false note somehow. She took her time. Should she tell him about the steam shovel and the government men searching her mother's suitcase at the bomb site? Looking for what? The same thing as he?

"A manuscript," she said. "Remember, he's an English professor, so there was always lots of paper around, but the entire building was levelled. Everything destroyed. I survived because I was lucky and I was all the way downstairs, in the part that's below ground. What kind of manuscript are you looking for? And tell me about the writing project you say he asked you about."

He didn't like that. She could see it flickering across his face for an instant.

He sat back again, shook his head and said, "Never mind. It's not important."

"Isn't it? What exactly is it that you do, Patrick?"

"A straight question. All right. I am the Canadian liaison officer with your OIC, the Operational Intelligence Centre, about events on the Canadian East Coast. The Russians have a naval presence there. They were our allies in the war, and at the moment we are still in close co-operation."

This felt right, and she was tempted to believe him. She said, "I have a photo album of your time at Oxford. The four of you. Picnics, and in a rowboat on some lake or large pond. Mum in a bathing costume, trailing a hand in the water. And one of her by candlelight, so beautiful. And then the wedding and my baptism."

"Ah, the wedding, yes."

For a brief moment the same look was in his eyes that she had seen the day she said goodbye at the tea room. Kindness and something else, something hidden.

He said, "I was Trevor's best man, Kate. Perhaps no one ever told you. David and I tossed a coin. We were all such good friends, including your mother. She worked in the dean's office, and she was often helpful. We all liked her a great deal. We called her Rose, our Rose of Tralee. After her favourite song."

Which was also true. There was even a gramophone recording of that song in the suitcase. Claire loved it too, and sometimes they put the disc on the turntable and hummed along with it:

> The pale moon was rising above the green mountain,
> The sun was declining beneath the blue sea,
> When I strayed with my love to the pure crystal fountain,
> That stands in the beautiful vale of Tralee . . .

Suddenly she wanted to leave. Withdraw, escape. And she knew why. It was because he had been best friends with her parents and she wanted to trust him, wanted to turn to him as the last surviving member of the group.

"Kate," he said. "Since you can't give me your number, let me give you mine."

He took out a small notebook and wrote in it. As he did so she watched him closely. Should she tell him about the secret room and the manuscript? Let him help her carry the burden? No, absolutely not. David had been very clear about that. Apart from that she also believed that trust had to be earned. Built up, bit by bit.

He finished writing, tore out the page and pushed it across. "The first number is here in London, and the other one is in Canada. The last name is Bailey, in case you've forgotten. Major Bailey for these numbers, and just Patrick for you. Okay?"

She nodded.

"Meanwhile I'll ask around about David's disappearance. If anyone will talk honestly to me. Kate, even as this war is barely over, we're already slipping sideways into the next conflict. The fight for world domination. The American atomic bombs on Japan a week ago were a signal for that. A harsh signal to the world about who has the absolute power and is ruthless enough to use it."

He pocketed his notebook and pen, and sat back in his chair.

"I'm glad we met today, Kate. And I'm very sorry, deeply sorry, for everything that's happened to you."

She took the page from his notebook, folded it, and put it in her handbag. As she did so she saw him looking at her hands. Early on in her mill job she'd tried to hide her hands from people, now no more.

She put her hands flat on the table for him to see in the window light.

"The new me," she said. "I lost my positions at Paramedics and at the horse farm. Much to my regret, because I loved those jobs. The bomb on our house did that too, robbed me of them and gave me the injury on my face. Now for the past few months, for sixpence an hour, twenty hours a week, I've been working at the mill as the machinist's helper, with oil and grease. I wear gloves, but they're cheap cotton. At the end of each day I scrub with Sunlight soap, but it's black graphite grease and it gets into the pores and small nicks in your skin and you can't get it out, no matter how much you scrub. But you know what? It's a small price to pay. The job came at the right time and it's good for me."

He looked at her hands and shook his head a bit and looked up at her and said nothing. Which was the right thing to do, and so for a moment she quite liked him again. She thanked him for the tea and pushed back her chair.

———

When she came home she looked at herself in the bathroom mirror. Made herself stay there, remain and endure, see her actual face and not look away to the wall behind her. Her cheek perhaps finally now allowed to heal in peace. She used the puff to wipe facial powder over the yellow bruise from the drained haematoma, but then wiped it off again.

In the garden, she hurried past the stone angel and on to the tree house. Today it would be just the two of them because Barbie was in London, at the conservatory.

She parted branches and stepped through them, and he was there. Late afternoon. A dim light inside, seemingly more substantial than the light outside. When she came in he looked up at her and smiled, and he patted the wood floor beside him. They lay back and stretched out and she shifted down a bit and rested her head in the crook of his arm.

"Thomas is gone, Eddie. Yesterday Claire and Dr. Elliott signed the papers, and the men from the institution came and took him away. The house feels so different with him gone. It was a hard decision for Claire. I know that. But what a relief."

She kissed his cheek and snuggled close to feel his warmth. "And just now I bumped into Patrick Bailey, David's friend. I told you about him. He insists he has no idea what happened to David and that he also didn't know about the bomb. I'm not sure I can believe him. And there's more: before that, I had an interview with the matron at Riverdale about a job at Physiotherapy, and there's a chance I'll be getting full-time work. She might even send me on a course in London. Maybe the rule about hiring only returned soldiers doesn't apply to them. She should know; she's in charge of all the support staff there, all the nurses and trainers. I'll find out tomorrow. The mill job was good for me, I always knew that. And my bosses were good to me, too. I'll wait till I know for sure, but this may be it."

"Katie, that's great! Full-time work, and training for it. Congratulations. And the horse farm?"

"Nothing, for now. I asked her once, and I'm not ready to ask her again."

"Not fair, is it?"

"I don't know. She says it wouldn't be fair to Anne either, and I can see that. Straight as an arrow, the woman. Oh, and one more thing: now, with Thomas gone, Claire wants to give a party for my birthday. I want you and Barbie there, of course, and maybe that man Patrick too."

"A birthday party. Good. I've got some news as well. I wrote the exam for the second level and now, if I pass, comes the third level, when I'll actually get to go up in airplanes as more than an observer. Up, up in the air, Katie. Some of that might be in Scotland and then in Canada, where I'll get to fly myself."

"In Canada?" She sat up and looked at him. "You're not leaving, are you?"

"No, no. Not *leaving*. Maybe just for some of level three. A few weeks. Probably. Come, lie down again."

He leaned on his elbow and bent over her. Ran his finger over her cheek and lips. "I'll have to go soon. But before I do, I need to tell you that I love your face."

"In this poor light."

"In any light. I love it. Period. Everything about it and what's behind it."

"Do you?" She closed her eyes. "Do you? In that case, can you stay a bit longer? I'm so happy right now."

Twenty-one

AT RIVERDALE the matron called Kate to her office and told her that the physiotherapy job was hers. In two weeks' time she'd be sent on an intensive training course in London, and then she'd be on probation for one month. If her work proved satisfactory, the job would become permanent at ninepence an hour.

When she told Dr. Elliott, he was pleased. He said physiotherapy was important work; the kind of work that women, in his opinion, were better at than men.

"If you like," he said, "until they send you to London, you can help out in my front room. Margaret will show you the ropes and it'll free her for other duties. Our cases are nothing compared to Thomas's pathology, but they'll help you get past him. All right? I'll clear it with Matron."

She asked him about her hands, her fingernails, and he looked at them.

"Talk to Margaret. She sees worse here. She'll probably suggest soaking your hands in warm turpentine and scrubbing gently with a soft brush. Soak and scrub repeatedly. It'll dissolve off. Then wash well, and when your hands are dry put on some lotion and work it in. Margaret will help you."

In the front room her job was taking patients' names and setting up their files. Every day she had to deal with more and more patients. Silent people who refused eye contact and were reluctant to answer simple questions. In time she was able to take them in fully and see them up close, begin to see the courageous side of them, men and women who'd given themselves a firm push and made the decision to come out and seek help. There was always a great stillness in the waiting room.

Sometimes at the end of a day Dr. Elliott talked to her.

He was helping them heal their minds, he told her. Or wait, he said. Their souls, more likely. If one believed in that. Not many did anymore, but he still did. Not in the religious sense, but in the human inner need sense, he said. The lostness and the yearning for meaning and structure, which was surely why humans had created their gods and all the stories trying to give substance to them.

He said that mostly all he did was sit still and listen. People often healed themselves by talking. Sometimes, especially in the early sessions, after a bit of prompting he said nothing more for the entire time. Perhaps a few guiding questions, but often not even that. Not another word until the long pause at the end, which was like a slow and relieved intake of breath. He just listened and let them feel that he understood and cared.

Twenty-two

THE SECOND TIME she met Patrick was the Sunday after V-J Day, August 15, 1945; Victory over Japan Day. He'd left a message for her with Tony, and they sat at one of the sun-dappled metal tables in front of the tea room. If she looked closely at the rust spots she could convince herself that it was the same table where the three of them had sat nearly a year ago.

"You look different," said Patrick. "Don't say anything. Let me guess. Your hair, right?"

She nodded and reached up to feel her hair, shaped and layered again the way she liked it. "I had it done the other day. Shampoo and a cut. I found the woman who used to do it for me. She's not that far away."

"It's nice. And all grown in?"

"Mostly. What did you find out about David?"

"Nothing yet. I made a few calls, but no one knows anything. Culture and Recreation is still only a part-time desk, and David's name didn't register with anyone I spoke to. But I've only just begun. In the meantime there is something else that's important. The reason why I left my message." He smiled at her.

"What?" she said.

He reached into his pocket, took something out and put it in front of her. It was a small box nicely wrapped and tied with a ribbon.

"You have an important day coming up and I don't know when I'll see you again. Happy birthday, Kate."

She looked at him, surprised and pleased. "How did you know?"

"Look at the pictures in Mary's photo album. I've known you all your life, Kate. I was even there at your baptism. St. Giles' Cathedral in Edinburgh. David was your godfather, which seemed only fair since I'd had the honour to be Trevor's best man. And you, dear Kate, you didn't give one cry, not a peep. You just kept looking earnestly at everybody, taking your time as though you were in charge of the entire thing and weren't too sure whether to approve of it or not. Like you are with me now, or at least were the last time."

He nodded at the present. "Open it."

She untied the bowtie, undid the wrapping, and opened the little box. It was a necklace, a fine gold chain with a gold pendant in the shape of horse's head within the outline of a heart. It was so lovely and so unexpected, her eyes stung. She held it and looked down at it. It was perfect. She could hardly believe it.

"Like it?" he said.

"I *love* it. It's beautiful. Thank you." She put it down carefully and got up and walked around the table and surprised herself by giving him a hug.

When she was back in her chair she picked up the necklace and opened the little clasp and with both hands reached behind her neck and put it on, tucked it into her blouse and looked at him. She felt the pendant new and solid against her skin and she liked the feeling.

"All good?" he said.

In the kitchen that evening Claire looked closely at the necklace. "It's beautiful. Eighteen-carat gold and so finely made. Who is this man? Tell me again."

"He and David were my parents' best friends at university. He is a major in the Canadian military and he liaises with our military. Something to do with Operational Intelligence."

"Really. *Patrick*, did you say?"

"Yes. Patrick Bailey. Why?"

"Oh, nothing."

"He said that maybe he could help me find out about David and Toronto and Reykjavik, but so far he hasn't found out anything. I'm still not one hundred per cent sure about him, but maybe now I'll give him another chance."

"Why not invite him to the birthday party?"

"We could. Let me think about it."

Twenty-three

THE BIRTHDAY PARTY took place in the living room. Claire had scrubbed the last bits of tape off the windows and had strung chains of coloured paper rings. There was white cake with decorations and a green number twenty-five on it, and a lit candle. Barbie, Edward, and Delbert were there, and so was Patrick; Kate had called the London number and left a message with her invitation. He was in civilian clothes again, in jacket and tie, and he'd brought two bottles of a sparkling wine from a vineyard in British Columbia. Claire popped the cork and poured glasses, and they toasted Kate.

Eager to play Claire's piano, Barbie sat down at the keyboard and played "Happy Birthday," and they all sang along. Then Barbie said, "While we're in a singing mood . . ." and she played a few bars of a tune. "This is on Radio Luxembourg at least twice a day. You've all heard it. Doris Day and her 'Sentimental Journey.' Come, sing along." And she began to play.

Halfway through the second verse Kate's voice failed and

she couldn't help it, and when Barbie saw her sitting with her cheeks wet but still trying to smile and sing, she almost stopped but then she carried on and they kept singing. But not for long. Soon the music and the singing stumbled to a halt and they all gathered around her, trying to hug her and endlessly asking what was wrong.

But she couldn't say, or didn't want to say. It was all too complicated, but wasn't it obvious anyway?

She wiped her cheeks with the back of her hand and was angry with herself. *Enough of this now. Enough.* Patrick handed her a folded handkerchief from his top pocket, but she shook her head and turned away.

She stood up, blew out the candle, and cut generous slices of cake and put them on plates. Delicate white Sèvres plates; like much in this house, still from Claire's piano-making mother Hélène, and from her grandmother long ago in France.

She sat with Edward and watched them eat and chat, Claire and Patrick leaning towards each other in easy, smiling conversation like newfound friends.

Barbie, clearly in love with the piano, kept playing song after song, and with a wink at Kate played some of their church basement songs now. "Carrickfergus," and then "The Rose of Tralee": . . . *'twas the truth in her eyes ever dawning / that made me love Mary, the Rose of Tralee . . .*

———

Then it was getting late and Kate wanted them all to leave so she could get Claire away from Patrick and spend time with her alone. She had intended to let him see the Oxford photos, but now she no longer felt like it. She whispered to Barbie, "Enough. Give them a hint and send them off with something."

And Barbie grinned and swallowed cake and wiped her fingers on a napkin. She sat down at the keyboard and called, "Last song and last drink, dear people, time to go home." She began to play "Goodnight Sweetheart," and soon they all sang along.

Later Kate and Claire sat at the desk in Kate's room. She'd put a new bulb into the lamp and straightened the shade, and now in its yellow light they looked once more at the photos in the Oxford album. Patrick and David and her father and mother, all so young. Still full of tomorrows and roads yet to travel. And something else between them. Something in who sat closer to whom. Something in their looks caught by the camera. In their smiles . . . but what?

She'd already studied these pictures again and again, had touched her fingertips to them like a blind person trying to decipher what was hidden there. Picnics under shade trees and on riverbanks. The wedding. Her baptism, there it was, and there was Patrick.

She tried to describe David's expression when Patrick had shown up at the tea room, and again when she left. As if there'd been something that David was being forced to do but didn't want to. As if he'd been pleading with her to understand, or to forgive him. *Yes, that*, she said to Claire. *For me to forgive him.* That was how she saw it now. So strange. It weighed on her, it still did. Forgive him for what? And where had it come from if it hadn't arrived with Patrick? There was something hidden about the man, she said to Claire. And something deeply unsettling about that last moment.

"Maybe," said Claire. "But I have to tell you, I quite liked him."

"I saw that. I saw you dancing with him."

"And I saw you with Edward. He cares about you, I can tell."

"Can you? I'm glad. What were you and Patrick talking about?"

"Many things. He told me about where he lives. Halifax is not far from where my mother lives in Nova Scotia, maybe two hours by car. Anyway. I saw his face when you turned down his handkerchief. Why did you do that?"

"Because I didn't want him drawing attention to me. Sitting there in my chair and wiping my eyes. I was just sad and happy and confused, Claire. In a private mood but a good mood too, among my best friends, and he was a stranger. He should have known that and kept back."

"If you put it that way, perhaps yes."

"All and all it was a difficult evening for me. Both wonderful and difficult, and I thank you for arranging it. Thank you, Claire. I learned something tonight. Or learned it *again*."

"You did? What?"

"That I need to get past all this. Start all over with a new life for myself. Get clarity and move on. And I will. Next week I'm off to London on that physio course."

In dreams that night, Moira in her wet clothes stood up from the planks across the millrun and took Kate by the hand and led her to the secret room. There was a great fire blazing in the room, but neither the desk nor the manuscript nor the corkboard were being consumed by the flames. Moira took off her coat and spread it near the fire. She shook out her wet hair and dried it in the heat, and dried her skirt and her blouse while her little baby bump showed and shadows danced on the walls. When the fire had burned down, Moira dressed in the near-dark, then she leaned and beckoned and gave Kate a kiss on her marked cheek. Moira raised a hand and gently brushed that cheek and instantly the scar was gone.

Then she walked out the door and down the street through the yellow pools of light from the street lamps, her solitary shadow lengthening and shortening and lengthening again. Becoming smaller and smaller until she was gone from view altogether.

Twenty-four

AFTER SHE CAME BACK from London, Kate worked in the equipment room at Riverdale, helping men with exercises for their war-broken bodies.

"You are good at this," Dr. Elliott said to her one day after he'd watched her work with a man on the spring tensor to regain flexibility in his knee. "And believe it or not, that scar on your cheek actually helps you. Especially when you pay no attention to it and you keep your chin up and your mind on the job. As you are doing. People see that and they admire it. It's what they want for themselves."

"Really? I'd like to believe that."

"Believe it, Kate. Believe it."

One day she rode her bicycle out again to the horse farm. A fine day, with the air getting colder now but still wonderful on her face and in her hair. The fields golden and the leaves on the trees in full colour and beginning to fall to the ground. Pyramid oaks, maples, cider apple trees, chestnut trees.

Wheeling around the last turn in the road she saw Mrs. Fitzhenry in her hacking jacket and riding breeches and boots, holding the braided riding crop in both hands across her chest. She was walking the dirt road between the barn and the paddocks, and when she saw Kate she stopped and waited for her. The horses saw her too and Princess put her ears forward and whinnied and blew and came up to the gate.

Kate stopped next to Mrs. Fitzhenry and climbed off the bicycle.

"I thought I told you not to come back here, Kate. Unless I called you."

"You did, Mrs. Fitzhenry. But that was months ago. You also said that I should be paying you for the pleasure of riding Princess, and today I wanted to tell you that I'm prepared to do that. I have good work now, and I can afford it. And look at her. She wants me to ride her. She's eager. Just look and be honest."

"*Be honest*, what nonsense you talk, girl."

But Mrs. Fitzhenry did turn to look at the horse stepping and turning impatiently at the gate.

"Why not let Anne continue with what she is doing now," said Kate, "and I come regularly to exercise Princess. Just her. She's doing so well, becoming so responsive. You could come along one day and watch us."

Mrs. Fitzhenry looked back at Kate. Studied her face, saw the scar on her cheek but did not stare at it. The hair all grown in, wavy and nicely shaped in a short cut. The way she stood in her fall jacket and American jeans and lace-up boots, holding the bike.

"This is quite forward of you, Kate. When I told you to stay away. What makes you think you can just come here and demand things?"

"I'm not demanding, Mrs. Fitzhenry. I'm simply asking."

"But why? When I told you not to come back."

"Because it's important. A last chance."

"Last chance for what? For whom?"

"Well, for me. You might have changed your mind."

Mrs. Fitzhenry half turned again and looked at the horse and then back at Kate.

"Princess is a strong and wilful animal, Kate. Do you really feel quite recovered? Fit enough to ride her?"

"I do. Absolutely. And I know her well."

"And how much would you be willing to pay for riding her? Let's say per outing. This is very unusual, you realize, and I'm in no way saying that I'm prepared to do it. But how much? I'm interested."

"I was thinking maybe ninepence per outing. I'd groom her afterwards, too. For free."

"Ninepence." Mrs. Fitzhenry kept studying her. There was something new in her expression, a surprised interest.

"I was paying you sixpence an hour, wasn't I? What sort of full-time job is it that you have now?"

"I work with demobbed soldiers in the physiotherapy room at the Riverdale Annex. Many of them after surgery on arms or legs. Under the senior therapist there. They sent me on a special course in London."

"And they pay you that well?"

"They pay me the going wage for a woman with some training. One pound fifteen a week. And I have some savings."

"Would you come every day?"

"No, not every day, but I could manage three times a week."

"It would have to be the same days every week. A regular routine, exercising and grooming."

"I could commit to that. But I couldn't feed her and wait, so someone would have to feed her an hour and a half before I come."

By now there was a hint of a smile on Mrs. Fitzhenry's face. So rare, and so good to see. She stood slapping the handle of the riding crop into her left palm a few times. Thinking.

"All right, Kate," she said then. "Here it is: you won't have to pay anything, and you won't get paid anything either. But you'll have to be punctual and reliable. Miss it just once without a good reason and a telephone call well in advance and it's all over. We'll feed her and you can use our tack. Sharpen Princess up for the auctions. You can walk her in the show paddock then too."

"Will she be sold? Really? I'm sorry to hear that."

"Sooner or later all our horses get sold. You must know that by now. This place has to pay for itself."

"Yes, I do know. Thank you, Mrs. Fitzhenry. It means a great deal to me."

"Good. Enough said. You can go now and say hello to Princess. I'm guessing that little bulge in your jacket pocket is an apple, is it?"

At home she put up the bike and then walked into the garden towards the tree house. Fall colours here too, orange and yellow leaves on the stone table and around the stone angel. At the tree house she parted the branches and ducked inside. Dark in here, the light nearly lilac. She sat down tailor-fashion on the wood floor and took a deep breath and closed her eyes.

Barbie was away, working in central London, in a piano shop where the owners let her practice on a Bösendorfer concert grand as much as she wanted, after hours. Not just once a week as at the other place. They'd also installed a special light to shine down on her and the piano so that people walking by in the dark could see her behind the wide window glass that had only recently been replaced. Barbie had said that often they stood in groups on the pavement, passing a thermos of tea while listening to Elgar and Chopin and Beethoven and to their wartime songs. These days the song they liked best was "We'll

Meet Again." Now, after the war, "We'll Meet Again" seemed to have become a song of acceptance, a farewell to loved ones who hadn't come back or had died in the bombings. One night when Barbie had played it, there'd been maybe a dozen of them out there in the semi-dark. Mostly women, Barbie had said. Probably war widows, and a few men. One of them began to sing along, at first a bit halting, then others joined in and soon they all stood singing in the dark, some of them with glistening cheeks.

Edward was in Scotland on the special aviation course he'd qualified for. He might be going to Winnipeg in Canada soon, to fly over their wide-open prairies. He hoped so, and he was excited about it, and by now she hoped it too, for him. He called her sometimes in the evening and told her about his day and she told him about hers. He said he loved her, and she listened to his words and took them in and kept them there in her heart.

She opened her eyes and looked around.

They rarely met here anymore in person, but their spirits were still here. As was Moira's. Her picture was still here too, a bit curled and wind-blown, but firmly pinned to the wall. All the memories of their first three seasons and of the beginning of their friendship in the tree house. So good, so important to remember.

Twenty-five

CLAIRE HAD SEEN Patrick's face when Kate refused his handkerchief at the birthday party, and had felt sorry for him. She thought he wanted to help for reasons much like her own, because he liked Kate and had known and liked her parents, and surely after all she'd been going through she'd need and accept help.

In addition, there was something about him that she found interesting. Likeable. Attractive, even. And not just his looks. This meeting now might help her see and feel more clearly.

She walked along the basement corridor at Riverdale to the canteen for doctors and nurses, and there he was, sitting with his back to a concrete pillar, sipping something from a cup. When he saw her, he put down the cup and stood up and readied a chair for her.

"Sorry I'm a bit late," she said. "We had an emergency."

"I won't keep you long. What can I get you?"

"They make a decent coffee here. Black, two sugars."

At the counter the girl drew the coffees from a large percolator and put two lumps of sugar on each saucer. He carried them to the table, set them down, and pushed his other cup out of the way.

"Smells good. I didn't know they had coffee here."

"It's a secret. Without strong hits of caffeine this place couldn't function. We lost far too many doctors and nurses in the war, and until the next generation is ready many of us need to work twelve- and fourteen-hour days. It's probably the same in Canada."

He nodded, and she saw him look her over quickly. Her hair, probably in some disarray, the white coat, the stethoscope in her pocket. Her left hand with the ring still on her finger and she didn't know why.

"So," she said to him. "What's this about? I feel a bit guilty about this meeting. Kate doesn't know about it and I don't like having secrets from her. She also thinks you are back in Canada by now."

"I will be, in a few days. But I wanted to come back to Gregor Mendel and his laws of heredity and genetics. Did you look him up?"

"No, sorry. I know you mentioned him at the birthday party, and I remember him from school, but not in any great detail. Just tell me."

Not far behind him she could see the wall clock. Most of the tables were empty because it was not lunchtime yet.

Dr. Jackson, the anaesthesiologist with whom she was sched-
uled in the operating theatre today, sat alone at a table holding
a cup with both hands.

"How much time do we have?" said Patrick.

"A few minutes. Ten, fifteen. Enough for a coffee. So what
about Mendel?"

"Right." He pushed his cup aside. "Did you ever meet
Trevor?"

"Kate's father. Yes, I did, and I also met David a few times,
because Mary was a patient of mine. We became friends and
along the way I learned her story. I liked her."

"Learned her story?"

"As a physician. What did you want to tell me?"

"I liked Mary too. A great deal. All three of us did. As you
can probably tell from the Oxford photographs. Remember
her hair? Black and shiny. Beautiful hair. Trevor had very dark
hair too. David's hair colour, on the other hand, that reddish
blond. Remember?"

"I do. Vaguely."

"Anyway, this is where Mendel comes in, because of Kate's
hair colour, chestnut-gold. See what I mean? How is that
possible?"

He had her attention now, if only because she suddenly
knew where he was going with this. She glanced at the clock
and looked back at him. "Tell me, Patrick. Get to the point.
Actually, I think I know what it is, but tell me anyway."

"The point, yes. It's a long story but I'll make it short. Kate has no idea. And as you know, she adored Trevor. And when he was killed, well. I heard about that, of course, and I heard from David how much it affected Kate. And Mary. Which was why he left Canada and moved here."

She raised a hand and said, "Stop. If this is what I think it is, and let's say I don't know, why do you think you have the right to tell me?"

He looked at her. Absolutely astonished. "Have the right? You know?"

"I do. The bare facts. Mary confided in me early on. I know she never told Kate. They were going to tell her at some point, the three of them together. But it never happened."

"Exactly. *The bare facts*, you say. Would you perhaps like to know a bit more background? For a fuller understanding."

He waited and when she made a vague gesture, he said, "Mary's parents, especially her father, did not like David. That is putting it mildly. Her father was a top-level civil servant. A man with a condescending look and a cane and a twirled moustache. For him David was a subspecies, a colonial, God forbid, from a place good only for lumber, mineral exploitation, and beaver pelts. He would never have agreed for his daughter to . . . well, you get the point. Mary knew that, and so when the situation became clear, the four of us—I should say the three of them—made a deal. Had to make a deal."

He paused and picked up his cup.

"Mary cared that much for what her father thought?"

"She did. In those days all daughters from good English families did. Marrying a colonial to be carried off to some frozen hinterland? Unthinkable."

"I suppose so. In those days, as you say. From her I know how she felt about the outcome. The *deal*, as you say. And everything else. Hated her father, hated having to leave her job and Oxford."

He nodded. "There were many tears and hugs, and in the end the plan, the agreement, was that she would marry Trevor, and David could not come forward until the child was twenty-one. Then the three of them would sit down and tell him or her, if by then they felt it was the right thing to do. But it had to be all three of them, together, in agreement. Well, by the time Kate was twenty-one, Trevor was dead and David was living with them here, and he didn't want to tell her."

"Because she'd loved Trevor as her father?" said Claire.

"Yes. He respected that. I was Trevor's best man at the wedding, and our Rose of Tralee was pregnant and only the four of us knew it. It was our secret. Later, once he'd done the math on the short pregnancy, Mary's father never forgave Trevor. He's the tall, sour guy in the baptism pictures. But tiny Kate, that day . . . I told her how good she was at the ceremony. Not one peep out of her. And her earnest little face." He sat back. "So you knew all along?"

"Most of it, yes."

She glanced at the wall clock. Over at his table Dr. Jackson stood up. He saw her, smiled and pointed at the ceiling. He picked up his cup and saucer and carried it to the counter.

Patrick said, "I was hoping you would help me think it through, Claire."

"Think what through?"

"Well . . . telling her."

"*Telling her?* What makes you—don't even think of it, Patrick. It's none of your business. And none of mine. Do you think she'll trust you or like you more if you tell her? Why would she?"

He stared at her.

"She won't, Patrick."

She looked at the clock again and back at him. Impatient now with him. Annoyed, even.

"I have to go. Kate has become a very dear friend to me. She's an amazing young woman, Patrick. Strong, considerate, and brave. How could that bit of confusing information, irrelevant even, possibly help her? What is it that you want from her? Are you after some sort of information about David? Or after something he was working on?"

"No. Why would you ask that?"

"Because that's what Kate thinks." She pushed back her chair and stood up. "This is actually upsetting me and I don't want to deal with it right now. Let it go, Patrick. It is absolutely none of your business."

"Earlier you said you don't like having secrets from her. This isn't a secret?"

"Yes, it is one, and it's also much more than that. It's about respect and love and courtesy. It's all that, and it's none of my business." She made a move to turn away.

"Wait! Claire, please wait. What about when David comes back?"

"If and when David comes back, it'll be wonderful for Kate. The rest is up to him. End of story."

"Claire, please sit down again."

"No, I can't. I need to scrub up and get ready for a procedure. We'll talk some other time."

"Can I call you?"

"From Canada?"

"Yes. Can I?"

She stepped around the chair and began to walk away.

"Can I?" he called after her. "Claire!"

And she, several steps away already, considered looking back at him over her shoulder and perhaps nodding, but then she didn't. She lowered her head and simply kept on walking.

In the lift she took off the ring and dropped it into her coat pocket.

Since Thomas had been committed to Scarborough Manor she'd been there once, for a meeting with the administrator about money. As she was leaving, Thomas had seen her from far away in the corridor, and he'd advanced and raised his fist and started cursing her. She'd backed away but he'd kept coming until two male attendants caught him and pushed him down into a chair. Later that same day she could suddenly do it: she called her lawyer, and not long thereafter her application for divorce was before the London Quarter Sessions of the Peace. The decree nisi stated a financial condition that she was able to meet, even if it was almost half her savings. She called the administrator at Scarborough to let him know that she'd opened an account in Thomas's name and had deposited the required amount of one thousand pounds in it.

The court declared the decree absolute and appointed a social services person to the case. If and when Thomas was discharged, Claire was to be informed and social services was to assist Thomas with his reintegration.

From Dr. Elliott she knew that his treatment included electroconvulsive therapy, and she also knew that the doctors at Scarborough called his case mildly promising. She was glad about that. If lithium were to become necessary, it would be an end of sorts, because while lithium did flatten the curve and calm patients, it also more or less demented them.

In the scrub room she turned off the taps with her elbows, then dried her hands and stood with her arms out while a nurse helped her with gown, gloves, cap, and mask. She took a deep breath and walked into the operating theatre. The bright lights were on and the patient lay on the table. Dr. Jackson was just completing the intubation.

Twenty-six

THREE TIMES A WEEK, as she'd promised, Kate bicycled to the horse farm. To make up her time in the physio room on those days, she worked late. She loved riding her bike to the farm, going fast in third gear. The whir of the spokes and the solid contact with the paved road through seat and handle-bar. In fields, crews were bringing the harvest home; lines of reapers making their way forward, the binders following them, and the binders in turn being followed by groups of local women and children picking up their leazings.

As it had turned out, for some reason to do with Anne's hours, Kate's job on those days wasn't just exercising Princess but also feeding all the horses. Sometimes Mrs. Fitzhenry helped, but most days she didn't.

"Sorry about that, Kate," she'd said the first time. "I know we hadn't planned on it, but Anne—never mind. Thanks for helping out."

After exercising Princess, Kate put her into cross ties and groomed her with currycomb, body brush, and hoof pick. Baby Horse, she called her. "Watch out, Baby Horse, move over. And watch your big feet. And stand straight for me, perfect posture like for the judge. Straight legs down from your shoulder, through your knees, and into your feet. Let's see you do it."

And Princess would blow and do her low rumbling nicker and nibble Kate's fingers with her lips.

"Why does she have to be sold one day?" she asked Mrs. Fitzhenry. "She's such a good horse."

"I know that, Kate," said Mrs. Fitzhenry. "I know how you feel about her, and I promise you that when the day comes and she leaves us, she won't be the last horse you'll take to. Not that that helps any. We all love this, all of it, but it's a business, Kate. And in money terms and risk terms, not even a very good one, to be honest."

One early morning, sitting with Claire in the kitchen over tea and toast with strawberry jam, Kate finally told her about the secret room and the manuscript. She described it all and told her about David's concerns and her promise of secrecy to him.

"But it's been more than a year now," she said, "and I don't think he'd mind. Not with you. I would never tell anyone at the college, or Patrick, but I don't want to keep it from you anymore. It bothered me all along."

"A secret writing room of his own, how interesting. I'd like to see it. Can I?" Claire looked up at the kitchen clock. "Now? Could we, Kate? Tomorrow I'm not on until three, but then for the next few days I'll be very busy again."

They put on coats and hats and boots and drove there. A cold night with spits of rain on the windshield. They parked out front and waited in the car for a few moments.

"Just to make sure no one followed us," said Kate. "I always do that."

In the room she closed the curtains and turned on the desk lamp.

Claire stood and looked around. "Interesting. And what's all this, the chapter cards?"

"Yes. The working title is *Dostoyevsky and Friends*. Friends more in David's imagination, in spirit. Rebels and freethinkers like Nietzsche and Kierkegaard."

She knelt at the loose boards, worked with the letter opener, and lifted out the manuscript with both hands.

"That's how much work he's done already. Almost four hundred pages in draft. And at the end of every chapter there are these annotations."

She untied her knot, took out the pages at the ends of the first three chapters, and showed them to Claire. "All handwritten in Cyrillic. Russian, I imagine, like private notes to himself. Patrick hinted at some writing project that David had wanted his help with, but when I asked him about it he wouldn't say. And so I don't believe him, don't trust him. I think he's after this manuscript or the chapter cards. Or maybe just after these handwritten pages that follow every chapter. I don't know why, but I have that feeling. Others may be after them too, like the men we saw at the bomb site, and later they went through the suitcase."

"But why? If it's just a literary piece of work."

"I don't know," said Kate.

"And in case he disappeared he wanted you to tell no one about it and burn it all. Why would he think about dying or disappearing?"

"That's just it. And all that on the very day when he knew that Patrick would be showing up. There was his face, Claire, his expression that I cannot get out of my mind. Regret, sorrow. Asking me for forgiveness, I keep thinking. But forgiveness for what? He never did a single bad thing, and he was such a good person to know. To talk to. Smart, and with a sophisticated sense of humour."

Claire took the pages of handwriting. "If you want to find out what this says, let me borrow it. My friend Annabelle knows a translator who reads and speaks Russian."

Kate thought for a moment, then she said, "It's tempting. Maybe not a whole page. I wouldn't want to give away too much."

"So copy just a line or two."

"All right. It might tell us something."

She sat down and copied two lines as best she could and handed the page to Claire. Then she tied up the manuscript and put it back into its hiding place, next to the pistol.

"And what on earth is that?" said Claire.

"It's something I got from Delbert. An investment. I did three twenty-pound runs for it, but he says that in a little while I'll be able to sell it for two or even three hundred pounds. I believe him."

She put the boards down, fit them precisely, and stood up.

Claire said, "I can see your dilemma about your promise to David. And while we are telling secrets, there is something I need to get off my chest as well. I want you to know that a few days ago I had coffee with Patrick. He rang me up."

"He did? Why? What did he want?"

"I think just to go for a coffee with me before he left for Canada. We met in the canteen at Riverdale."

"You like him, don't you? Admit it. Were you afraid to tell me?"

"Yes and no. *Yes.*"

"Don't be, Claire. Maybe when you get to know him better you'll find out things that'll make me trust him. What did you talk about?"

Claire shrugged. "Not much. Coffee chit-chat. I only had a few minutes."

"Come on, Claire. What did you talk about? You have that look on your face."

"What look? It was just chit-chat, really. Nothing important."

Out in the dark somewhere, they could hear a car engine starting up, then shutting down again. Men's voices. Silence.

"Let's go home," said Claire. "I'm suddenly very tired."

Twenty-seven

CLAIRE SENT THE PAGE with the copied line in Cyrillic to Annabelle's office, and on the telephone she explained about Kate and David Cooper; his foreign assignment to Toronto and Reykjavik, and now his disappearance. This page might hold a clue.

Two days later Annabelle rang to say she had some information. They met and drove down to the embankment in Claire's car; a damp London day with mist rising off the river, shrouding the bridges. They sat in the car with their coats on.

"So," said Annabelle. "Two things: the Russian text and David Cooper. Culture and Recreation is still more or less shut down, but I managed to get a look. Last October there was an entry with his name, but it said nothing about Reykjavik or Toronto. His official destination was listed as Leningrad, and the assignment came from Canada. From their East Coast station. All costs to be borne by them."

"Leningrad. To what purpose? Did it say that?"

"No, it didn't."

"Did it list any contact over there? Like a case officer?"

"No. But I did look into the East Coast station, and it's in Halifax, Nova Scotia."

This took a moment to sink in. "Halifax," said Claire then. "Really."

Halifax was where Patrick had said he was stationed, because of the Russian presence there. Was he lying to her as well? She started the engine and turned up the heater to help clear the windows.

"So was it easy to find out? For anyone?"

"I wouldn't say *anyone*, but for someone who knew her way around and had at least my level of clearance, yes."

So it would have been possible for Patrick too. Maybe he hadn't been looking at all. Maybe he didn't even need to, because he knew.

"Is that bad news?" said Annabelle. She looked at her watch.

"It's puzzling news, in a way. It may confirm Kate's suspicions about David's friend. What about the Russian text?"

"Yes. That's just—I'll show you. It could in fact be nothing more than notes for a work of fiction."

Annabelle took two pages from her coat pocket. She unfolded them.

"Here is the original back to you, and this is what it says in English. I typed it up. It says, *lives in a rented room in Anna Ketov's house and in case he moves she will* . . . That's all."

Claire skimmed the line. She shook her head, folded the pages and put them away.

"So when can I meet your Kate?" said Annabelle.

"Anytime you like. Come for dinner. How about Sunday? I'll even open my last bottle of pre-war French red."

"Deal," said Annabelle. "Now, let's go. We can talk while we drive. How is your mother?"

"I think she is fine. I know she wants me to come and visit, and I'd like to. If I can arrange for some time off."

"Time off? With your busy schedule?"

"I know, but there's someone I'm training, and she's doing well. She could take over for a few weeks, and it would be good experience for her. Kate could come along and visit David's horse farm. We'll see."

At the Sunday dinner Kate listened to what Annabelle was saying. Leningrad made no more sense to her than Toronto or Reykjavik, and the fact that Patrick might not have made an effort to find out anything made her glad that she hadn't trusted him. The name Anna Ketov did not appear anywhere in the chapter where the page had been. She had read it twice and had written down the name of each character, but they were all different, and the reference to a rented room did not fit either. Not so far.

"This is very good, Kate," said Annabelle. "I understand you were the cook."

"I was. Thank you."

She'd made a stew and had served it along with potatoes and peas from her garden. There was a white tablecloth on the table, and Claire had brought out the good linen napkins and her mother's silverware.

For a while they ate in silence, then out loud Kate suddenly said, "But why? I mean Leningrad. What for?"

Annabelle looked at her across the table and said, "Leningrad is still some sort of intellectual centre, going back to the days when it was called Saint Petersburg. And your David is a university professor, a cultured western Russian-speaker and writer with access to academics and intellectuals. Maybe our side is using him to get certain kinds of information."

Like her dad. And it proved to be his fate. It was possible. Was it?

Twenty-eight

A WEEK LATER the matron at Riverdale called Kate to her office and asked her to sit down.

"There have been developments, Kate. It's bad news, and there's no good way to say it. Until now the government didn't interfere with our hiring practices, but suddenly that's changed. They increased the quota, and now . . . well, I have to replace you with a demobbed soldier. There it is."

"You are letting me go?"

"It's not that I *want* to. I have no choice. It's happening everywhere, with so many men still coming home from field hospitals and places."

"But . . ." The shock of it. The disappointment.

The matron waited. Then she said, "I'm sorry, Kate."

"But you trained me for this. Especially. And I thought I was good at it."

"You were. And you still are."

"So?"

"Ex-service people have top priority."

"Is he trained?"

"I don't know. Even if he is, we'll have to bring him up to speed with the new machinery. The senior therapist will do that."

"So can I at least keep my job until he's ready? Or can I coach him on the machinery?"

"Sorry, no. It's over, Kate. You get a good reference and an extra week's wages, but that's it."

Claire tried to console her, and so did Eddie on the telephone and Barbie in person. Their kind words helped, but not very much. The loss felt enormous to her.

At the horse farm Mrs. Fitzhenry looked at her and shook her head and said she was sorry to hear it. What made it worse was that the horse auction was only days away, and Princess was one of the five horses to be sold.

Kate asked Mrs. Fitzhenry for permission to spend the night before the auction on the cot in the empty groom's cabin in the barn, and Mrs. Fitzhenry thought for a moment. Then she nodded and said, "All right, Kate. I understand. Dress warmly."

She didn't sleep much that night, but she did not mind. Whenever she was awake she could hear the horses rumbling in their sleep, could hear their hooves shifting as they stood up from an hour or two of deep sleep to continue dozing on their feet. Once in a while she got up and tiptoed over to Princess and sometimes saw her on the ground and sometimes saw her standing.

"Baby Horse," she whispered to her. "Go lie down and get some good sleep. You've got a big day tomorrow."

Back on her cot in the dark and with her eyes closed she said goodbye to her short career as a physiotherapist. And at the same time she knew that this too, everything around her right now, was exceptional and a privilege, however hard-earned, but somehow like everything else it too might soon be coming to an end.

So enjoy it and use it up, she told herself. *All of this. This cot, the barn smell, the sweet hay, the horses, the sounds. Princess. All of it, breathe it in while you have it, Kate Henderson.*

In the morning she broke the skim ice in the tank, washed up, and combed her hair. Then she put on her good jeans and the boots and her winter jacket. An hour before the showing she groomed Princess with brush, comb, and body cloth until she gleamed.

"Baby Horse," she said to her. "Walk well and true today. With pride and snap. An elastic stride, and no dwelling and no sideways motion. You know how to do that. Right?"

And Princess nickered and rumbled and nibbled Kate's hand with her lips.

Out in the yard lorries with horse trailers were pulling up

like an enemy army, and people stood in small groups by the rails around the show paddock, talking and sipping tea with steam rising, waiting for the auction to begin. Cold and sunny out there, with an early dusting of snow on the ground.

"A perfect day," Mrs. Fitzhenry said when she came by to inspect Princess. She was dressed in knee boots and breeches and her tweed hacking jacket. "Good, Kate. She'll be number four. And she's counting on you to lead her well. Figure eights, remember. That'll show them everything they need to see."

"Yes, Mrs. Fitzhenry. I know."

When it was nearly their turn Kate snapped on the short lead line and walked Princess to just inside the barn door. She ran her hand over the horse's neck. "I'll miss you," she said to her. "I really will."

Princess rumbled and stepped, excited by all this commotion, and then the auctioneer raised his bullhorn and announced number four.

"And now, ladies and gentlemen . . . Princess! A fine six-year-old Morab. Let's see her."

Kate tugged at the lead line. "That's you, Baby Horse. Come. Let's do it."

And they moved out the gate at a good pace towards the centre pole in the paddock to begin their first figure eight.

Twenty-nine

"SO WHERE IS EDWARD?" asked Claire. "You haven't mentioned him in a while."

"He's still in Scotland. Learning to fly. It's the third stage of his training. Canada is next. The prairies. That's coming soon, and he's looking forward to it."

"And then?"

"Then I don't know. We'll see."

Claire said nothing for a while. In the silence, the clock on the wall ticked. It was four fifteen in the morning and they were in the kitchen having tea and their favourite, toast with strawberry jam.

"So someday soon he'll be a pilot."

"That's his plan," said Kate. "Always was. It's what he wants more than anything else."

"And you? What would you like to have happen when he comes back?"

"Mostly I'd like things between us to remain as good as they are now. Maybe make a bit of progress."

"Progress?"

"Well, you know. Not marriage just yet, but at least some clear understanding of where we're heading. Something to build on."

"Of course. Clarity. From what I've seen, men and women can have very different ideas, unspoken ideas, of how they want to live their lives. What they would like to have happen. Sometimes they don't want the same things deep down, and if they don't say so then things can go wrong. Often with blame and hard feelings on both sides. But I'm sure you know all that by now."

"I do know that. But I think it's different with Eddie and me. I'm in a bit of a difficult situation right now without the physiotherapy job and Princess, but I'm working on it. I think Eddie and I, we know what each of us wants."

"That's wonderful, Kate. I'm glad for you. Still, there's something I think I should say to you. Can I?"

"Of course."

"Do you know any military wives?"

"No."

"I do. With all these bases around, I always had a number of women patients that were married to pilots. There may be some who don't mind moving around all the time, from country to country and base to base. But the ones I knew hated it. Living out of suitcases and among cheap used furniture all the time. Forever trying to befriend other army or air force wives because they were lonely. Especially the ones with children, they really hated it. I know that's not what you want to hear."

"No, I don't mind, Claire. And I know all that. Or I think I know it, but we're not there yet. And it's too negative. We'll just have to see. But I am aware of the possibility."

"Good. Enough said. And speaking of travelling—I had a call from Patrick today. At work."

"You did? About what?"

"He wanted to tell me about a new trauma centre that's going up in Halifax. A brand-new hospital with all the latest technology, and apparently they are looking for doctors with my qualification and experience. Probably for very good money, too."

"Claire! What are you thinking?"

"Only that we could take a trip, you and I. There is someone who could fill in for me at work, and my mother really wants me to visit. I'm sure she'd also like to meet you. So we could do that, and I'll take a look at the hospital and you take a look at David's horse farm. No plans to stay, just a nice little change and maybe to give ourselves options. Legally the horse farm is probably yours by now. Isn't that what the lawyer said?"

"Something like that. But I'd have to go to court and get a ruling that declares David lost and in all likelihood dead. And just the thought of it . . . I couldn't do that just yet."

"No. But would you want to come to Canada with me and look around a bit? Meet my mother? We can't stay with them because their place is too small, but she'll ask the priest and I'm sure he'll let us stay in the flat up in the church annex. Probably you could see Edward too, while we're over there."

Kate said nothing to that for a long time. She sipped tea and crumbled a piece of dry toast on a plate with her fingers. Princess was gone and she was not needed at any job right now—not *wanted*, really. And the other day Delbert had said that there would be maybe four or five more runs at most. Demand was still there and prices were high, but supplies were drying up. And she did not want to ask at the mill again. It wouldn't seem right. That job had been perfect for her at the time; now it would be a step back, when it was perhaps time to look up and go strongly forward. And she had money now. Quite a bit, actually. She was contributing her share to the household and she felt good about that.

"Kate?" said Claire. "How about it? A trip to Canada? I'd really like to go."

Kate dropped the piece of toast and rubbed the crumbs off her fingers.

"I'm thinking maybe yes, Claire. I've always wanted to see Willowbank, the farm, ever since David told me about it. They have wild horses there, did I ever tell you that? There's a wild herd on the adjoining Crown land, and every year the government vet tells them how many and which horses to cut out of the wild herd to keep it stable. And they are allowed to keep those horses. Anyway. Can I sleep on it?"

"Yes, of course you can."

Thirty

ON HER WAY to a consultation at the Royal London Hospital, Claire took a shortcut through the grounds of Scarborough Manor. To her surprise the car park was deserted, and as she drove past the main entrance she could see that the tall wooden doors had been chained and padlocked shut. She continued driving around the building to see if there were any open doors or windows, but there weren't. Another entrance at the rear was also chained shut through the door handles.

When she told Dr. Elliott, he said he hadn't heard of the closure, but he'd look into it. Two days later, standing in the hallway outside his office, he told her that yes, funding for Scarborough had unfortunately run out and the place had been closed.

"Just like that? Can they do that?" she said.

"Well, yes. I understand it wasn't voluntary. The charity pulled out first and Council couldn't, or didn't want to, carry the place on its own. So it was closed."

"But what about the patients? What about Thomas?"

"Apparently a proper medical assessment was made of each patient. Some were taken in by other hospitals, some were deemed incurable and sent to Farnsworth, and quite a few were discharged. Thomas was."

"Discharged! Was he that much better?"

"Must have been."

"Was he ever on lithium?"

"I didn't ask, Claire. Not my place. It would be in the file, which is of course sealed."

"Of course," she said.

They stood by a tall window. A grey sky out there, grey slate roofs with pigeons hunkering near chimney pots for warmth.

"All right, Claire?"

"Yes, all right, John. Thank you. Do we know where Thomas went?"

"I didn't ask, but the court-appointed social services person should know. In fact, as I remember, they should have informed you."

"Yes, they should have. I'll find out."

"You do that. I have to go, Claire. It's one of those days for me." He smiled at her and started to turn away, but then he changed his mind and came close again.

"Is everything all right?"

"I hope so. It's just that I was so relieved that he was out of my life and was getting treatment. I don't want him suddenly knocking on my door again."

"No, of course not."

She looked down at her hands, fiddling with the car keys. The shock of it. *Not thinking clearly right now.* She looked back up at him. "But thanks for letting me know, John."

On the telephone from her office, social services said that Thomas had been taken in at the hostel on Basil Street in the north end of town.

"You were on our list to call, and we would have gotten round to it eventually. Sorry, there's quite a backlog these days."

"I understand. How long can he stay there?"

"As long as he wants," said the woman. "Some stay for weeks, others for years. It costs next to nothing. Some of them have no other plans and they stay until they're carried out feet first."

But this was not to be the end of it. Only two nights later, during a shift at Riverdale, Helen at the front desk came hurrying to tell her that there was a man in the car park shouting and pounding on her car with his fists.

Claire ran downstairs and stepped out the main entrance, and in the lamplight she could see that it was of course Thomas.

There was a cold rain coming down, and he was out there dressed ridiculously in shorts and a short-sleeved shirt, pounding the roof of her car. She yelled at him to stop, and immediately he turned and came charging. She stepped quickly back inside and Helen helped her bolt the heavy door.

"Call the police, Helen. *Now. Please.*"

He was standing out there in the rain and she could see him through the glass panel in the door, soaking wet and pounding the door now, yelling, "You bitch, open the door or I'll break the glass and reach in and drag you through it, I swear. Open up, open up now!" For a while he was using actual words, then he went back to just screaming with spit flying from his mouth, and all the while she stood there by the locked door, conflicted and frozen with horror.

Mentally unstable and extremely dangerous had been Dr. Elliott's succinct final summary in layman's terms.

"They're on their way, Dr. Giroux," said Helen from behind her desk. "When we call them, they're always here very quickly."

And never had Claire been more relieved to hear a police siren in the distance coming closer and to see their signal light flashing in the night.

They were two policemen, and Thomas swung at them and dove and punched, but they managed to cuff him and put him in the back seat of their car. When it was safe, Claire unlocked the entrance door. One policeman stayed with Thomas while the other took her statement.

"Your ex-husband, you say? Will you be pressing charges, Dr. Giroux?"

"No, I won't. Let's go and look at the car."

The policeman walked with her to inspect the damage. The roof and the bonnet were dented in places, but nothing was broken and the dents shouldn't be too hard for a body shop to repair.

She said again that no, she would not be pressing charges. "Just keep him away from me."

"A restraining order? You'd need to go to court for that."

"No, I don't want to go to court. I want him out of my life, not finding his way back in through some court case."

"We can keep him locked up for tonight, but if there are no charges we'll have to let him go in the morning. A restraining order would give you legal protection, Dr. Giroux."

"Legal. Look at him. Do you think he cares about legal?"

When Kate learned about the nighttime event, she went to look for Delbert at the Elgin. He was in, playing chess with another man at a table in the hall. When he saw her he said something to the man and stood up and came her way.

He motioned her to follow him outside and then they stood among the bare trees and bushes by the back door.

He said, "When's Eddie coming home?"

"Very soon. But only for two days. *Two days!* Then he's already off again. To Canada. And there is something else."

He looked at her. Waited a bit. "What is it, Kate?"

And then he stood in silence while he listened to her about Thomas.

Late next afternoon Claire was still at home when Delbert came to the house and rang the bell. Kate let him in. They sat in the dining room over tea with milk. Slices of toast stood in a little silver cooling rack, and butter and jam were nearby. Delbert helped himself freely. He looked well. Clean-shaven and with a good haircut, in a jacket and white shirt and a good pair of trousers.

He told them that he'd asked around about Thomas, and it turned out that someone—not at the Elgin but at another shelter—had heard about him. Certain rumours in connection with him.

"What rumours?" said Claire.

"Well . . . not good. Rumours about a fragging. That's how serious. And it's because of the fragging that the fellow remembered the name. The men in Thomas's platoon must have really hated him."

"Why? What's a fragging?" said Claire.

Delbert made a tossing motion. "Hand grenades. Fragmentation. I know for a fact that it was done even to officers. Young asshole lieutenants, excuse the expression. In the noise and confusion of battle, toss a grenade and no one will ever know or question where it came from."

"Really?" said Claire.

"Yes. Really."

"But that's a horror story. And you think they did that to Thomas? It would explain his injuries. Several in his back and the backs of his arms and legs from what I could see. Each maybe half an inch or an inch across."

"Sounds about right," said Delbert. "He was lucky it didn't kill him. Or unlucky. The things I saw, Dr. Giroux, what a lot of us saw and went through . . . terrible."

There was a pause and then Kate said, "Like what, Delbert? What did you see and go through? Can you talk a bit about it? To help us understand."

Delbert looked at her. He put his slice of toast back on the plate and sat still for a long moment. Then he said, "I never told anyone, not even Edward. He never asked, but you just did and that's important. So all right . . . an example. The main single experience for me happened in a small town halfway up Italy, a town with a very old church and a convent. Narrow cobbled streets and house-to-house fighting. We lost many men there."

He picked up the toast, then put it down and looked at Claire and Kate. He sat back in the chair.

"That day the convent got shelled. Maybe by mistake, or maybe on purpose, to cause confusion. We never knew by which side—theirs or ours—but that day I saw nuns and novices in white habits and wimples all bloodied running in the streets, crying and praying. Nuns and novices, faithful brides of Jesus, as the romance goes. Are you sure you want to hear this?"

"Does it have to do with Thomas?" asked Claire.

"It all does, with all of us. What we went through and how some of us came out of it. Or didn't. You want to hear it?"

They said nothing at first, just sat looking at him. Then Claire said, "Please tell us."

"All right. So, in a street I saw one young nun. Her arms full of something. At first I didn't know what it was, maybe a wounded child, but then I saw that she was trying to hold in her intestines. Pink tubes and blood. In her white habit all ripped open and bloody, the white wimple tight around her face. I'll never forget that, never."

They stared at him.

"It gets worse. I picked her up, crossfire and artillery shells all around us, and I ducked and carried her inside a house entrance, thick walls and a stone floor there where I thought she'd be safe while I ran to find a medic. And I did find one, but by the time we got back to her she had died. You see . . ."

He paused and closed his eyes for a moment. He opened them and said, "It changed my life, that event. That one hour, it did. And, really, where was my brother's God when he let it happen to her? It's too easy to say he took her home, much too easy.

Dying is normal, we all die, but this was murder. No, worse. It was indifferent slaughter. I can imagine of course what Walter's church would say, about testing her faith. All those made-up notions. But all during that hour and before . . ."

Delbert shook his head. "There's much I'm not saying outright, but it's there, isn't it? Apart from all that, and as for my own guilt, rather than run off to find someone to help her live, in her condition with her pain and fear and with the unbelievable horror all around, I should have stayed with her, held her hand and helped her die. As a kind fellow human being, that's what I should have done. Broke my heart, to find her gone. To have failed her. It did."

There was a lengthy pause. The sun was on the horizon now, casting an orange light into the room.

He sat forward.

"That is my convent story. It changed me in ways that are difficult to describe, and for a while it was hard to carry on." He shook his head to himself. "Some days it still is. I'm a structural engineer by profession and the City of London has offered me a job in rebuilding, but I told them I need some time. For this, among other things." He nodded his head. "For this, mostly. Some space, a bit of time. But it's interesting to hear myself tell it out loud to someone. It's good. I've never done that before, not to anyone. Thank you for asking, Kate."

They all sat in silence for a moment, then he stirred and said, "Is there more tea?"

Kate stood up and poured him another cup. She pushed milk and sugar closer.

"Thank you," he said. He spooned in sugar. "Now, in terms of helping you with Thomas—"

"Do you really think he was *fragged*?" said Claire.

"Probably. From what the fellow heard, and the way you describe his injuries."

"What could he have done that his men hated him so much?"

"Be a bad leader, for one. Put his men in unnecessary danger. Be a coward and risk their lives rather than his own. Men can read one another in an instant. They can." He nodded, then he said, "I'm prepared to talk to him, Dr. Giroux. Warn him off, man to man. Just talk, mind you, for now, but making it clear that if he doesn't stay away from you—you get my point. It'll make an impression. Guaranteed."

Delbert spoke calmly, firmly. He looked at Kate and said, "I'd make him understand that if he causes any more harm to either of you I know where to find him. He'll get the idea."

For a long moment they all sat in silence in the darkening light. Banks of orange clouds on the horizon and distant trees in sharp outline against the sky.

"I should go," said Delbert. "But about Thomas . . . if you want me to talk to him, you need to say so, just so we're clear."

He drained his cup and set it down past the spoon in the saucer and looked at them. Waiting.

Thirty-one

WHEN KATE AND EDWARD climbed out of the taxi, Park Lane was busy with cars and pedestrians. Windows gleamed and flags rippled, and a line of horse-drawn coaches was parked along the pavement.

At the hotel the uniformed doorman smiled at them. He reached for the polished brass handle and pulled the door wide open.

She had booked the room the previous day, and now she just picked up the key. They took the lift to their floor, and in the hallway in front of their room she made him close his eyes. She kissed him on the lips, turned, used the key, and opened the door.

"You can look now," she said.

The room was wonderful. Elegant furnishings and floor-length drapes. A king-size bed and a view of the park out the window.

———

All during their stay at the hotel, they made love more often than she would later be able to remember. They luxuriated in the bathtub and romped some more in the bed, smelling of the good soap and the shampoo. They laughed and had pillow fights.

They took their afternoon tea in the room, and their dinner at a candlelit table in the dining room. After their first few sips of wine Edward took out a small jewellery box and pushed it across the table. She watched his face as he did that, his shyness but his thrill also, and she loved him all the more for it.

The ring had a small bright stone in it, and it was beautiful. She put it on and got up and walked around the table and gave him a kiss.

After dinner and back upstairs they sat close together in the chairs and looked out the window. The park was in darkness now but around it hundreds of lights glimmered. In the street the yellow cones of car headlights slid past, and on horse-drawn coaches the bench lights were on and lit tail lanterns dangled.

They spoke about what was coming. She was tempted to press him for details. What about the longer future? What about marriage, what about children? Where would they live and how did he see all that fitting in with his own plans? A military pilot, what did that mean for a little family?

But she decided to wait and not to crowd him; to keep it simple for now and to let it show itself.

"Do you think I can visit you in Winnipeg?" she said.

"I don't see why not. I'll find out about it and let you know."

"How far is it from Nova Scotia?"

"I don't know, but Canada is a big country."

"You can write to me at Claire's mother's address in Nova Scotia. I'll be there for maybe one or two weeks and then I'll travel to the horse farm. I'll give you that address too."

"*Your* horse farm."

"No, it's David's. I haven't done that yet. And I can't. There is something that . . ."

Edward waited. Then he said, "Something what? Go on."

She considered changing her mind and still not telling him, but then she stood up and turned her chair to face him, and she told him everything about the secret room and the manuscript and her promise to David.

"*Wow*," said Edward. "Amazing. Who'll look after it while you're away?"

"Nobody. It doesn't need looking after. It's closed up and secret. That's what he asked for, and except for the landlord and Claire and now you, no one knows about it. I think he'll be back one day. I can feel it, Edward. Perhaps I just really, really want to feel it, but I think it's true. Sometimes when I sit in the room and look around, it's as if he were there with me."

"I know the feeling, Katie. For the longest time after we got the news about my dad, I felt he was still there with us."

He was silent for a while, then he said, "And I think he *was*, too."

Next day she showed Edward the room and the hole in the floor with the manuscript and the Beretta. He stood looking at it all, astonished.

"A man's secrets," he said. "And now yours."

She rearranged the floorboards in perfect alignment and checked the window once more to make sure it was locked. She took him home in a taxi, but not long thereafter she came back to the room because there was something she needed to do alone.

She took off her coat and sat down at the typewriter.

```
    Dear David,

    Edward is here and he's already packing his bags
    again to go to Canada. And in little more than a week
    Claire and I will be leaving for Canada as well; she
    is making last-minute preparations for that at
    work. I look forward to our trip. I'll go and visit
    Willowbank and I'm sure I'll see Eddie over there.
    I'm excited about it all. He is flying on an RCAF
    transport plane, but Claire and I will be travelling
    on a ship, a freighter that was commissioned to
    take military equipment back to Halifax. The ship
    is called the Sackville. It has only six passenger
    cabins. We'll be eating at the captain's table and
    we'll celebrate Christmas on board too.
```

I've told Tony that I'll be away for a little while,
maybe for a month. No more than two. Some of it
depends on what we're going to find over there, and
maybe on Edward's training as well.

Edward and I are engaged, David. ENGAGED! Sometimes
when I look at him, I love him so much and I feel
so close to him that it actually hurts my heart.

Tony knows that I want to keep the room, and I've
already paid rent for another year. And by the way,
I finally told Eddie and Claire about your secret.
You've been gone a long time, David, and with them it
started to weigh on me. It had become MY secret, and it
separated me from them and I didn't want that anymore.

Missing you,

Kate

NOVA SCOTIA, CANADA

1946

Thirty-two

IT WAS ALL SO DIFFERENT HERE. The cold ocean air. More breathing room somehow; more space between people and houses. No bomb sites, but great boulders and dolmen stones in places, as though the world had worn down around them, or the ocean had receded and taken the earth with it.

They were staying in a small one-bedroom flat high up in the church annex in Saint Homais, and sometimes in her first few nights there, Kate would do what she'd done in the kitchen in Claire's house in England. She'd stand at the window high up and look out onto another silver moon track, this one not on a river but on the mighty Gulf of Maine. New Brunswick was across the Bay of Fundy to her right; Bangor, Maine, lay far away in front of her, and the light in the sky more to her left would be from the city of Portland, Maine.

The other window in the room overlooked the town; moonlight on shingled roofs, brick chimneys, smoke rising from some of them, thin and straight into the night. The market square with the moon shadow of the church steeple falling across it.

She'd insisted that Claire should take the bedroom while she slept on the pull-out couch in the living room. She liked it out here. She could get up in the dark and walk around, look out the windows and crawl back under the covers and try and sleep some more. And then she'd be up again, careful walking around so as not to bump into furniture and wake Claire. She'd listen at her door, listen to the silence, glad that Claire was able to sleep.

The map she'd bought showed the Canadian East Coast only; Winnipeg was nearly two thousand miles west. By now, a few days after their arrival, she'd been at the post office three times already to ring Edward's number, but no one had ever answered. Disappointing, but time would tell. How hard could it be to find another number for his base in Winnipeg?

Claire's mother, Hélène, was an interesting woman; outspoken and strong-willed still. Apparently she had never approved of Thomas, had never held back about it, and she still did not. The woman also had quite a history; most significantly she had once killed a man. Had shot him through the heart with a large-bore rifle because he'd begged her to, when they were trapped in the wilderness and he wanted to set her free. There had been two court cases about it, the last one in this very town, and everybody knew about the killing.

Last night, during dinner, Hélène had studied Kate across the table. "A physiotherapist, a paramedic, and a horsewoman," she'd said. "That scar on your cheek. Was it caused by a horse?"

"No, it wasn't," Kate had replied, and said nothing more. She simply continued to eat. The pause following her words stretched, and when Kate looked up, their eyes met and Hélène coloured ever so slightly. That simple exchange and what they recognized in each other at that moment set the tone for their relationship.

In the morning Kate walked Claire to the bus stop for her two-day trip to the new trauma centre in Halifax. When she was back, Hélène made coffee and invited Kate to join her at the kitchen table. From somewhere they heard tap-tapping sounds, and Hélène explained that it was Mr. Chandler in his leather workshop, a room through the door at the end of the kitchen. She paused for a moment, then she said, "I shouldn't have asked about your scar. I apologize. It would be like people asking me about my limp."

"What limp?"

"Thank you. Have you been able to reach your friend yet? You can use our telephone, you know. No need to walk to the post office every time."

"No, I haven't reached him yet. There's never an answer at that number. And it's long distance."

"That's all right."

"Thank you. And I mean it: I don't see a limp."

"No? It was frostbite, that time in the wilderness. I have special insoles that sort of make up for the missing toes. Mr. Chandler made them for me. It was a long time ago and I've made peace with it."

"I'm learning to do that as well. The scar is from the bomb on our house. It was much, much worse. It disfigured me and I felt ashamed. I struggled with it for a long time. If it hadn't been for Claire—I don't know. Some days I'm still aware of it, but not so much anymore."

"Yes. I can understand that very well."

"Mr. Chandler works in leather?"

"Yes. We met soon after I came here. A long time ago. Before the court case. Claire will have told you about that. Has she?"

"Yes. The basic facts."

"The basic facts are all anyone knows and needs to know. The rest is for me to know and to deal with. It wasn't murder, Kate. It was an act of kindness. A most terrible act of kindness. For me. But as I say, I've made peace with it."

There was a pause, then Hélène said, "Mr. Chandler, yes. He helped me save myself. But enough of that. Let me ask Meg at the telephone exchange if she can find another number in Winnipeg. That little ring on your finger, is it from him?"

"Edward. Yes. We are engaged." She raised her hand and wiggled the finger.

Hélène smiled at her.

Two hours later another number had been found. The operator put Kate through and she was given yet another number. Not long thereafter she was finally speaking with Edward. He sounded far away and distracted, and there were loud noises around him. Voices and laughter, a crowd of men and women.

"Edward," she said loudly. "Eddie! Can you hear me?"

"Barely. There's an assembly going on. Some of them passed, and now they're in line for their wings. They're celebrating already."

She asked him if she should be coming out by train to see him, as they'd planned, but he said that now was not a good time. Next week they'd be flying north into wild country. And then to Regina. And then out west. He would let her know.

"Will you, Eddie? Will you keep in touch? I had a hard time reaching you."

"Sorry, Katie. It's a big organization and there's always a lot going on."

Among all the commotion someone called his name, a woman, and hurriedly he said, "I have to go, Katie, sorry. Someone is about to make a speech. Sorry. I'll call you. Where are you now?"

"At Hélène's mother's place. You have that number."

"All right. I'll call you."

"Eddie! Eddie, wait!"

But he'd already hung up.

While Hélène was at piano practice Kate walked the town in her coat and wool hat. Ancient cobbled streets and lanes. Stone houses and French names on mailboxes. Gables with dates carved into them, two hundred years ago and more. The cathedral with its dark wooden portal and stone gargoyles hunkering at the ends of heavy eavestroughs.

She entered.

Hélène was playing the piano at the front of the church, and perhaps two dozen people were sitting in the pews, listening to her. Some sunk into themselves, sitting with their eyes closed. Kate tiptoed forward along the centre aisle and sat down in a pew. Tall leaded windows and large, dark paintings of the stations of the cross on the side walls. The music sounded wonderful. What was that piece Hélène was playing? Kate had heard it before, probably played by Barbie. She sat back and listened, and soon she closed her eyes as well.

The walk hadn't calmed her, but now the music in this setting helped. She hadn't asked Eddie when it would be a good time to come out. Or had she, and he hadn't answered? Would he call on his own and let her know, or should she keep calling him? Wild country and Regina, indeed. He'd sounded different. Different, how? Not just distracted. Harder. Focused on something else entirely. *But let it go for now, let it go. Listen.*

Afterward she walked up to Hélène and asked her about that last piece she'd been playing.

"The 'Ave Maria' by Schubert. Did you like it?"

"I loved it. It was wonderful. I've heard it before, I think, played by a friend of mine."

"The friend who played 'Für Elise' for Claire and wanted to borrow my Molnar?"

"Yes. Her name is Barbie. In the end she never did borrow it. We couldn't find proper transport for the longest time, and then other opportunities developed for her. A sponsor, and now she's even touring. Short trips to towns near London, to begin with."

"Then your friend Barbie is fortunate. I think I was too. I grew up in a piano factory, and I took piano at a music school. I stumbled into performance when as a girl I had to demonstrate our pianos to company buyers. I think I have a bit of my mother's talent. But come, let me introduce you to my oldest friend in town."

When they arrived, Mildred, the owner of the Hôtel Yamoussouke, was at the front desk. She hugged Hélène, and

when Hélène had made the introduction, Mildred spontane-
ously reached and hugged Kate as well. She called a young
man in a hotel uniform to take her place and then led the way
to the dining room. She served coffee and croissants and sat
with them.

"Since day one, this one here"—she indicated Hélène—
"the day she arrived in town, the same day, she came and
rented a room. Very quiet, she wanted it, just trees and the
ocean, and that's what she got. A few days later there was a
funeral for three fishermen, and we all heard her playing the
church piano for the first time. The church was packed, *packed*
I tell you, and she played so very well. You tell her, Hélène,
what you were playing."

"I remember I started with the second movement of the
Brahms Requiem, and then I played the Navy Hymn. *O hear
us when we cry to Thee for those in peril on the sea.*"

"And that was the one that did it," said Mildred. "She improvised it into a drawn-out, wonderful tune, a rondo you might
say, and I'm telling you, Kate, we sat frozen in our seats, all of
us. We all knew the hymn of course, but we'd never heard it
played like that. So very fine. We'd all known the drowned men,
and this music, the way she played it, her phrasing, it made some
of us weep. It did. And I tell you, Kate, from that day on Hélène
was one of us. Simple as that."

———

Back at the house Mr. Chandler told them that there had been a telephone call from England. A man by the name of Wilbert or Delbert had called about someone by the name of Thomas. He was asking Claire or Kate to call him back, and he'd left a number.

The number was written in pencil on a piece of scrap paper, and Kate recognized it immediately. It was Delbert's number at the Elgin. It troubled her, and after she'd received Hélène's permission to use the phone she placed the call. She asked the operator to let her know the charges afterward and then stood waiting through the clicks and beeps.

Eventually somebody picked up. She asked for Delbert and heard the receiver being put down on a hard surface. "Delbert!" she heard someone call. "Hurry, man. Long distance. Canada." And then there was Delbert.

"Kate!" he said. "How are you, and how is Dr. Giroux?"

Kate filled him in quickly and then asked about the reason for his call.

"I just wanted the doctor and you to know that I had that talk with Thomas. You know, warning him off. But now, yesterday, when I asked at the shelter, they hadn't seen him in more than a week. And the social services woman who is supposed to be in charge of him hasn't seen him either. I asked her."

"So we don't know where he is?"

"Not at the moment. But I did talk to him. Clearly and strongly."

"What did you say? Did you threaten him?"

"I told him what would happen to him if he didn't leave Dr. Giroux and you alone. In pretty clear terms. He didn't say anything but I think it made an impression on him."

"So could he be hiding from you now?"

"It's possible. There are other shelters in London. I can ask around and let you know."

"He has to be somewhere, Delbert. I don't think Claire wants to see him ever again, but for her peace of mind she'd probably like to know where he is."

Claire was back the next day. "Should I worry about it?" she asked Kate. "Did Delbert sound worried?"

They were in the bedroom up in the church annex. Kate sat in the chair while Claire was unpacking her overnight bag. She took out the toiletries, put them in the bathroom, and came back.

"I wouldn't say *worried*," said Kate. "Just noting a fact. He thinks that maybe Thomas doesn't want to be found. But he said he'd ask around."

"So maybe he really is just hiding."

"Maybe. You can always call Delbert back in a few days. See if he's found out anything. How was the trauma centre?"

"It was fabulous, Kate. Lots of beds and all the latest equipment. There's new machinery that's similar to X-rays but it works with some sort of magnetic imaging. It's very promising for soft-tissue examination. I met the head of Trauma, and she's a woman! A Dr. Winters. And guess what."

"What?"

"I saw Patrick and we had lunch. A very short one, because he got angry and left when I told him we found out about David and Leningrad, and how easy it had been, so why couldn't he have found that out too?"

"And?" said Kate.

"He didn't like me saying that."

Claire held the empty overnight bag upside down. She shook it out, closed it, and put it under the bed.

Thirty-three

NEXT DAY CLAIRE DID CALL DELBERT. She made the call from the post office because she didn't want her mother listening in. She sat on the little swivel stool with her elbows on the metal shelf, telling Delbert that yes, she would feel better if she knew where Thomas was.

Delbert said, "I understand, Dr. Giroux. And I will try to find him, if only—as you say—so we know where he is and I can keep an eye on him. I did make things clear to him, about not harming you or Kate ever again. And so it's possible I scared him into hiding. I didn't mean to worry you, just to keep you informed. Maybe just let it go."

"I'll try. I'd like to."

"Good. Other than that, how are you?"

"I'm fine. Kate is too. She's gone to the horse farm. Left early this morning by bus to a place called Antigonish, where the farm manager will pick her up. In a week or two I'll visit her."

"Good. You are on a holiday, so remember to enjoy yourself."

"I will. That new trauma centre is fabulous. So advanced. And so many cases of massive injuries where I could be helpful. In a few days I'll take another look at it."

"You're not really thinking of letting them hire you, are you, Dr. Giroux? All your professional and private life is here. And we have massive injuries here as well. We've all been through the same war."

"How true," she said. "We'll see. Maybe it's mostly the Thomas problem that I want to get away from."

When she'd hung up the phone she sat in the booth for a while longer. Something else was troubling her: it was that failed lunch meeting with Patrick the other day, when she'd been on the tour of the new hospital and he'd shown up out of nowhere. He'd waved and come up to her and quickly asked her to meet him for lunch in the cafeteria.

"How did you know I was here?" she'd asked him, and he'd grinned and said, "I'm in intelligence. We know everything."

When they met she told him that she knew that David's real destination had been Leningrad, not Toronto and Reykjavik.

"And the assignment came from your East Coast station in Halifax," she said. "So you must know much more than you told Kate. And me. Why not just tell us the truth, Patrick?"

"Ah. The famous truth. What truth, dear Claire? Some things are much more complicated than they appear. There's a surface, and underneath there are multiple layers of facts and truths. Files with red labels. Call me in a few days. If I find out more, I'll tell you. In the meantime don't go suspecting and accusing."

He'd stood up abruptly, bumping the table. Angry now, showing a different side of himself. "Sorry, Claire," he'd said, and walked away.

Now the way she'd spoken to him felt wrong, and she wanted to make up for it. She walked to the operator's desk and gave her his number in Halifax.

The phone was answered by a man, and she gave her name and said she wanted to speak with Major Bailey. There were a few muffled sounds and then Patrick came on the line.

"Claire, I want to apologize about the other day at lunch," he said right away. "I overreacted and handled it badly. I do have a bit more information now. But not on the telephone. Can we meet somewhere?"

They met in the ferry parking lot in Caribou, more or less halfway between them; Claire had borrowed her mother's car to drive there. His tone of regret on the telephone had sounded sincere, and she felt regret as well. For some reason she still wanted to believe this man.

They sat on a bench in their winter coats, not far from the ferry terminal. A fine day in January; sunny and bright, but cold.

"Patrick," she said. "I need you to be completely honest. The moment I feel you're not, I'll get into my car and leave. Agree?"

"Agree, as long as the being honest part goes for you as well."

He stretched his legs and kept his hands in his coat pockets. At first he'd taken off his hat, but after a while he'd put it back on. Over to their right the ferry to Prince Edward Island was leaving harbour. Gulls swarmed around it and dove into its wake for food stirred up by the propellers. The ferry sounded its horn.

"So?" she said.

"So back then, the three of us signed up and swore an oath that is still holding. Even now."

"Back when?"

"A few years after the Great War. We were so young. David and Trevor and I. We felt honoured, Claire. Thrilled to be asked. For me, intelligence became a full-time career; Trevor went into politics and David became a teacher. A university professor. First in England, then in Canada, and for brief stints even in Saint Petersburg and Berlin, when they were looking for a native English speaker. David always was, *is*, academically the smartest of the three of us. And all along he also served as a special . . . let's say *envoy*. For Canadian interests, and now British interests as well."

He paused for a while and she sat still, waiting. Was Patrick for once telling the truth? She felt he was.

"They are using him as a fisherman, Claire. And it's true, on this last assignment I was his case officer, assigned jointly by our East Coast station and by your OIC. They used him that way in the past, and now even more so, with this war over and everyone competing for certain people to lure over to our side."

"Use him how? And what's a fisherman?"

"A fisherman casts his net. It's code for people we're using to identify scientists and other exceptional people, mostly in Russia and Germany, that might be willing to come over to our side. We're all doing that now, all the Allies. The Americans succeeded spectacularly with Wernher von Braun, the rocket specialist from the V-2 program that terrorized London. He was a brilliant catch for whatever fisherman landed him. A real boost for the American space program, to help them compete with the Russians."

"But David is just an English teacher," she said. "A writer. He wouldn't know any rocket specialists or other high flyers."

"No? How about literary high flyers? Or how about potential informants among like-minded intellectuals and dissidents whom he would have met at the conferences he went to? The nature of his assignments was always classified, of course, and classified several layers above the level that your friend Annabelle Spencer has access to. Yes, I do know about her. Look at me, Claire. Are you wondering why I am telling you all this?"

"Maybe because you said you'd be honest?"

"Yes, that too. But as you must know, honesty comes in all sorts of layers, with other layers withheld, as in a balancing act. No, the reason I'm telling you all this is to make you understand how complicated it is. Claire, I honestly do not know where David is right now. Our East Coast station deals mostly with Russian intelligence. We trade information, Claire. Carefully and selectively. And it's true we sent him to Leningrad, where he had contact with more than a dozen people we're interested in. All very hush-hush, Claire. We know that he did arrive and that he did attend some conferences and meetings, but then he disappeared. We don't know why, except that he may have information that is valuable for the other side as well, and dangerous for the people involved. I also think that he is in trouble because of it."

"What kind of trouble?"

"I don't know. But I do know his way of working, and I'm willing to bet he was compiling coded lists. And I would dearly like to know what's on those lists. Names, people's backgrounds, where they live, qualifications and other pointers. It would be in an embedded code, but I could deal with that."

"Would that be the document or manuscript that you asked Kate about?"

"Yes, it would be," he admitted. "Guilty as charged. I asked her straight out and she said she knew nothing about it. I don't believe that."

She looked away from him and thought about that for a long moment. As she did, she saw the bundled manuscript under the floorboards in David's secret room; the pages in Cyrillic, perhaps containing hidden identifiers about people, such as someone living in a rented room at Anna Ketov's. All that secrecy and coding, and then Kate's innocent letters to him pinned to the corkboard.

"And you, Claire," said Patrick. "Did she ever talk to you about such a document?"

"No, she never did." Claire shook her head. Amazed at how easy it was to lie in order to protect a loved one.

"I think she knows something," he said. "I could sense it. The two are very close. And since she won't tell me, I can only hope that she doesn't tell anyone else either. Ask her to do that, will you please? *Not to tell anyone.* It would seriously endanger David and certain other people, and not just his contacts. In some cultures people can simply disappear. Poisoned, or wrapped in anchor chain and dropped in the ocean." He paused, then he said, "Don't say that to Kate. You wanted the truth, now handle it with care."

The ferry was far away now, a dot on the northern horizon. A perfect sky, blue and cold with picture-book clouds.

"Yes, I did want the truth," she said. "And by now I'm almost sorry I asked for it. Do you think that's what happened to David?"

"Anchor chain? I wish I knew. I hope not. Actually, I don't think so."

She wanted to say more. To even this out, to explain Kate's reasons. She could say something like, It's because Kate really likes and admires David. And she gave him a solemn promise, and Kate is probably the most loyal person I have ever met.

Yes, she could say that, but it was not up to her, and the very strangeness of Kate's promise to David would only raise more questions. And so she said nothing more. Just sat on this bench next to him, worrying about all this and watching the ocean and the seagulls, and the waves breaking high against the rocks.

Thirty-four

AFTER THREE DAYS and nights at Willowbank, Kate moved out of the bedroom they'd given her and slept in a groom's bunk room in the barn, as she'd done for her last night with Princess. The bedroom had come to feel all wrong because at night the house creaked in the onshore winds, and the wood floor sounded as though someone were walking on it.

When David had lived here it had been his room, Mr. Anderson had told her.

"All the time as a boy and then a young man, until he went off to university in England. You could say we grew up together, right here. I'm the second-generation manager now, by a written agreement with David. My wife and I, we're eking out a small profit, which we're allowed to keep. Our son wants nothing to do with horses. He's studying engineering in Toronto, but I have deep roots here. My grandfather was barn boss when David's grandparents owned the farm. That's how long ago, Miss Henderson."

"Just call me Kate, please."

"All right, I will. Kate." He nodded. A tall, spare man with a lined face, grey stubble, short greying hair, and friendly eyes. He said, "You sure you'll be all right in the bunk there? There's more blankets and woollens if you need them. Nights can get cold. Can I ask why you want to sleep there?"

"I just like it better. I wear a sweatsuit at night and I have enough blankets. It all works just fine."

Twice in her nights in the bedroom she'd dreamt of David, had seen visions of him, not as the boy who'd lived in this room and not as he had looked the last time she saw him, but much aged, and injured; once waking her up and standing there with blood on his face. Standing close, his face pale and still, just the blood flowing from his nose and mouth, and then in that dream he became her dad dying in her lap on the trundle path.

She woke with a scream and leapt out of bed with her heart pounding. Stood confused and terrified with his image still there, and there, and there, wherever she looked in the dark, and when at last it faded she still had no idea of where she was, and whether perhaps he had been real and was once again asking for her help.

The barn she slept in was sheathed with milled one-by-eight-inch red cedar. Mr. Anderson had explained that the boards weren't shiplapped but were nailed to the frame with narrow gaps between them that closed in the damp season when the wood swelled, and opened in the dry.

Inside it was clean and tidy and fresh-smelling, stall after stall. The stable end of it was empty during the day and occupied at night when the horses were brought inside. From her doorless bunk room she could hear them standing up or settling down and shifting their feet. She loved those sounds, loved looking around in the dark and seeing stars winking between the boards. Once in a while she'd crawl out from under the blankets and walk down the line of stalls, look at the dark shapes of the horses, half of them dozing while standing up with the stay apparatus of ligaments in their knee joints locked.

Mrs. Anderson had a kind face and brunette hair twisted up into a loose bun and kept there with combs and pins. She was good with the horses; Kate had seen that already. They both were. Kind but firm, and horses came to respect that.

She'd asked Mrs. Anderson to give her a job to do, so that she might earn her keep while she was on the farm, and that job turned out to be exercising and grooming horses. One of the horses was called Lucy. She was smallish, nervous, and coarse-haired. A cut-out, Mrs. Anderson said; cut out of the wild herd the previous year.

"It's our wild horses that make this place different, Kate. Like other farms, we too board people's horses for a fee, and we teach riding and let them use our horses. We also have a foal or two a year. But it's the six or seven wild ones we get every year that make all the difference. Like Lucy. She's all right with a saddle by now, but she's still a bit of a kicker. That's why we can't sell her yet. Never come up on her from where she can't see you easily. Just one good kick can kill a person, but you know that of course."

She did know that. For her first time with Lucy she took the halter strap from Mr. Anderson's hand, and when he'd stepped away she talked to the horse. She stroked Lucy's neck repeat-edly, then let her get the scent of her hand, taking her time. She didn't ride her for the first two days, just spent time with her in the stall, grooming her and talking to her. When Lucy was out in the paddock she'd sometimes go to the fence and bring her some hayseeds or an apple.

On the third day she saddled her and led her out of the barn. Mr. Anderson stood watching. She held the reins in her left hand on the withers and with the other hand held the near stir-rup and stepped into it, swung her right leg up and over, found the other stirrup, and gathered the horse.

"Nice," said Mr. Anderson. "The English way. We just hop on. Some of the cowboys that'll be here soon, I've seen them leap on a horse at a run. Want someone to come along with you?"

"No. Thank you. I think we'll be fine. I'm surprised, there's practically no snow here."

"Not yet," he said. "We've been lucky so far this year."

She called Edward's number several times. The first few times the phone just kept ringing and ringing. Then one day a man picked up and told her that Edward's squadron was out. She explained who she was, and he became friendlier. They were out west, he said. Practising in the Rocky Mountains. Which was very different flying, with all those thermals and thinner air in places and denser, cold air over ice and snow. Was there a message?

She said, "Yes!" Practically shouted it. "Tell him to call me! Remind him who I am and that he promised. He has the number but I'll give it to you again."

There was a dog on the farm, a female black lab called Tippy, and she and Tippy made friends. Tippy lived in a doghouse by the main building, and Kate would go there and fetch Tippy and take her for walks. Sometimes when the two of them sat in the tall grass by the eastern fence they could glimpse horses from the wild herd. They could hear hooves pounding.

She explained about wild horses to Tippy, and patted her, and Tippy slapped her tail and grinned.

She also called Claire several times. The first time, Hélène picked up and told her that Claire was in Halifax again, for another look at the trauma centre. Every time thereafter it was Claire who picked up.

One day Claire asked, "When would you like me to come and visit? I could stay a few days. Would be nice."

"Anytime. I miss you, but I also know that your mother missed you. So I don't want to get in the way. But I could come anytime and pick you up. There's an old Ford station wagon here. I could come tomorrow. See how eager I am? I could be there around eleven."

Claire laughed at that. She sounded happy. "So do it. I'm free now. Mother will understand."

"Really? Tomorrow?"

"Sure. On the way you can tell me all about the farm."

"It's different, Claire. Sad somehow. For me."

"Sad, why? Tell me, Kate."

"David, I think. Growing up here, then leaving for England for the best education, then coming back, teaching in Halifax and Toronto, and then when Dad was killed and Mum needed help, walking away from all this and hurrying back to live with us. I'll always be glad he did, but you'd have to ask why.

Such a big move. I'll tell you more tomorrow. We'll have lots to talk about."

"We will. I have something to tell you too. About Patrick and David."

"Tell me now!"

"No, tomorrow, Kate. We'll have more time."

Thirty-five

IN THE MORNING KATE FILLED UP the station wagon at the pump and then left for Saint Homais. Through small towns along the way, always reminding herself to keep to the right side of the road. Past white wooden churches and stone churches built a long time ago, and often a glimpse of the ocean to her right: Cobequid Bay, the Minas Channel, the Bay of Fundy, then a stretch of gravel pits with lorries coming and going. Enormous boulders the size of houses in fields to her left, tall white pines and bare trees, ravens with wingspans wider than she had ever seen.

At the house, Claire's suitcase stood packed and ready at the door while the four of them ate lunch at the kitchen table. Mr. Chandler admired Kate's English ankle boots. He kept looking at them under the table.

"Good calf's leather on those, and a good heel," he said to her. "An inch, is it? Inch and a quarter? Just right for walking, and riding too. A good hold in the stirrup, I bet. Is that what some call a paddock boot, or a jodhpur boot?"

"It is, Mr. Chandler. I love these boots. I bought them second-hand in London, but they're still in good condition. I look after them."

"Would you mind if I made a pattern from them?"

She didn't mind at all. She'd be pleased, she told him. And so, when they'd finished lunch she followed him into his workshop and sat on a bench and took off her boots, and then watched him take measurements and draw precise shapes on sheets of pattern paper.

An hour later they were off. Hélène and Mr. Chandler stood outside and waved. He in an old cardigan she'd draped over his shoulders. Hélène a bit subdued.

"Drive carefully," she called. "And bring her back soon, Kate. I don't see enough of her as it is."

She drove back the same way she'd come. After a while Claire said, "So, about your David—it's something Patrick told me. I met with him again."

"You did? When?"

"A week ago. Listen . . ."

And then for a long stretch of road she told Kate about fishermen and about David's assignment according to Patrick, and what those pages in Cyrillic script might contain, not that she had mentioned anything about the manuscript to Patrick. But the handwriting might be code about real people whom he was in contact with, and whom he wanted to protect.

Kate had slowed down. She was listening and thinking, but she also needed to pay attention to the road. At one point she pulled over and shut off the engine.

"It makes perfect sense, Claire. And in that case the reason why he would want me to burn it all if he dies or disappears would be to protect their identities."

"Could be, yes. Of course."

She started the engine and drove on. At the gravel pits there was heavy traffic again. She slowed down. One of the lorries, a large black one, stayed behind them for a long stretch. Eventually it overtook them in a roar of engine and tires. Behind the dust-smeared window she briefly saw the driver's angry face staring at her, perhaps because she was going too slowly. Then he was gone. But his face, his sneer, stayed with her a while longer. Something about it, something. *Could it be? No, it couldn't.* But for a moment the shock of the thought distracted her from what Claire was saying, and so she interrupted her and said, "Sorry, Claire. I wasn't listening just now. You were saying?"

"That those notes in Russian might tell you something, but you can't risk having more of them translated, because at home Russian-speakers are probably a small community and word would get round. Even if it's in his own creative code."

"Exactly. I wouldn't dare. How did Patrick seem? Do you think he's telling the truth this time?"

"I think so. He admitted that he hadn't been completely honest, and he apologized. He said I could tell you what he told me, but for obvious reasons you should keep it to yourself. *We* should."

"'Not completely honest' is an understatement, Claire. He was telling lies. Simple as that."

"True. But now you can understand why."

"I suppose so. But I still don't trust him. This could be just another story."

Claire said nothing for a while. Then she said, "It could be. Parts of it, anyway. I never thought of that."

They drove on. The Minas Basin to their left now. Golden in the late afternoon sun. An outrigger with its booms far out like a tightrope walker, balancing. Seagulls all around it. And then suddenly from the corner of her eye she saw the black lorry coming at them at tremendous speed from a side road on their right. For split seconds like flash frames she saw the massive front of the lorry, the wide steel bumper, the grille, the windshield like a mirror in the sun, and then felt the great bulk of it as it slammed into their car on Claire's side and pushed them around and rolled them, and that hard, dizzy spinning and the upside down and the blows to her head and body would be all she'd remember in nightmares and visions long afterward.

Thirty-six

AT ONE TIME she woke in a room all in darkness. She knew she did not want to be there, and so she spread her wings and rose up high and drifted away again. Next time she woke in a room bright with sunlight; she had no idea where she was and she had a terrible headache. Someone dressed in white with golden hair and golden sunlight on her shoulders was sitting by her bedside. A woman. Claire? She tried to say, "Claire, Claire? Where are we?" but her throat and mouth could not form the words. Then the woman looked up and she was not Claire.

Claire was in intensive care, in another room. That was all the nurse would say. Even four days later, on Kate's way downstairs to talk to the policeman, the nurse would let her see Claire only briefly through the half-open door. Claire completely still, with wires and monitors attached and with bandages on her neck and head.

The nurse tugged at Kate's arm and closed the door.

"What are her injuries?" asked Kate.

"You should ask Dr. Winters. And I did call the mother. They'll come as soon as the doctor allows it."

On the way downstairs in her hospital robe and slippers, Kate held on to the railing with her left hand, to the nurse with her right. She felt a bit nauseous and dizzy; she knew she had suffered a concussion and many scrapes and bruises. Claire's condition was obviously much worse.

Kate had learned about concussion in the paramedic course, and then had seen serious cases in the field. The physical injury and then the mental trauma; fear and shock lasting for weeks and months afterward.

She and the uniformed policeman sat in the visiting room, where there were chairs and tables. They were the only people there. She asked him to sit across from her because she had difficulty looking to the sides.

He said, "Of course, of course," and he picked up his notebook and changed chairs. An older man with his uniform cap off. Friendly.

"So could you tell me what happened?" he said. "I've been to the site and I've seen the station wagon. It was totalled. A massive side impact, and then rolled a few times. Can you describe the vehicle that hit you?"

"A lorry. Big and black. With a heavy steel bumper."

"A truck?" he said.

"Well, yes. Massive. Black."

He wrote in his notebook and looked up. "What else do you remember? Like the make of the truck? Or the licence plate? Even a partial?"

"No. It all happened so fast. But I caught a glimpse of the driver's face. Not at that moment but earlier, when he passed us. He was behind us for some time, but then he sped up and overtook us and drove off. And when he passed I saw his face, his expression. I didn't want to believe it, but he looked like someone we know: Dr. Giroux's ex-husband. She was in the passenger seat. The last time we saw him was in England. Then he disappeared."

"In England."

She nodded. "I know that sounds far away. But it did look like him. No, wait! That's too vague. I *know* it was him. I'm positive. That sneer. I know it so well. A big, strong man. Dark hair, black eyes. Thomas Braemar is his name."

The policeman kept writing. He looked up. "You were on the coastal road heading northeast and he came at you from the Barrington side road there? I saw the skid marks."

"Yes, and so fast. He knew exactly what he was doing. The road was bad there and I was driving slowly."

"Anything else you can tell me?"

"Not much. But look at us. The injuries he caused. I realize there are no fatalities, but you are going to look for him, right? For the truck. There'd have to be some damage on it."

"Oh, we'll look for it. And we'll keep you informed."

Dr. Winters allowed her to see Claire, briefly from the open door. She said, "When I took Dr. Giroux on her tours she mentioned that you are a certified paramedic. So you'll know the basics. She not only has injuries all over her body, which are bad enough. She also has serious head trauma, a deep laceration on her neck, and cracked ribs."

"But she'll be all right? Eventually?"

"I am hopeful. After her time here with us she'll need several more weeks for full recovery."

"Of course. I'll look after her. She can stay with me on the farm."

"Good. You, I should be able to discharge in a few more days, and next time you visit her you can probably sit with her. In a sterile coat and cap and gloves. I'll tell the desk nurse that you have my permission."

Kate stood in the open door and looked at Claire. So pale. So utterly exhausted. Eyes closed.

"Claire," she called softly. "Claire?"

"Don't," said Dr. Winters by her side. "Let her rest." She reached for Kate's arm and gently pulled her back and closed the door. "I know, I know. But she is making progress.

Her vitals are good and the numbers are getting better."

"When do you think she'll wake up?"

The doctor shook her head. "We don't know that."

Five days later, when Dr. Winters discharged Kate, the Andersons came in the farm truck. It was red and much smaller than the one that had hit them. They sat side by side in the cabin, Mrs. Anderson in the middle, with her feet in brown laced shoes to either side of the drive-shaft tunnel. She said that normally she'd wear a skirt for a city visit and especially for a hospital. But not today. Today she'd put on trousers knowing that Mr. Anderson would have to shift that long gear lever between her knees.

Mr. Anderson drove well. He was clean-shaven and he wore pressed trousers, a jacket, and a hat. His hands on the steering wheel looked callused and strong.

"Your poor doctor friend," Mrs. Anderson said. "When she's ready you must bring her to the farm to recover."

"Good. Thank you," said Kate. "I was going to ask you. She'll need a good rest."

"Well, of course. She can have the spare room on the main floor. The boys used it as their study. Nice view out the window to the paddocks, and the cowboys will be coming soon. Maybe rent a hospital bed for her."

For a while they drove in silence, then Mr. Anderson said,

"And completely out of nowhere, right? But it goes to show. You get up in the mornin' and you have no idea how the day will end. You think you do, but you don't."

She called Hélène from the telephone in the hall. Mr. Anderson saw her standing there and he brought a chair. She sat down. Exhausted, and her mind and her voice still not working quite as they should.

On the other end of the line Hélène said, "How is she? And what does the doctor say? And when can we come and visit her? A nurse called, but please tell me everything from the beginning."

And Kate did. Tried to, but had to pause often, and at times her voice failed and she waited and breathed into it and carried on.

"And you, Kate?" said Hélène.

She went for walks with Tippy and she groomed horses. She could not exercise them yet, not until her spells of headaches and dizziness had cleared completely, but within days she could think better and talk in connected sentences. She tried it out on Tippy, and Tippy looked up at her and grinned and wagged her tail.

And every day she called Dr. Winters at the hospital and listened to her about Claire's condition and progress. On the sixth day she said that she would like to visit Claire, and Dr. Winters gave her permission.

Kate had Mr. Anderson drive her to the bus station, and from there she took the bus into the city. She took a taxi to the Chevrolet dealership and there she bought a Chevy Fleetmaster station wagon for the farm, to replace the one she had borrowed and wrecked. The new one had wood panelling, an adjustable visor over the windshield, a brown front-seat bench, a chrome shift lever on the steering column, and enough room in the back "to move an entire household," the salesman said. She insured the car with the same company that held the other farm policies, and from the telephone on the manager's desk she called her bank in London and cleared the transaction. While the salesman was away to get her licence plate, she wrote a counter cheque on her London bank account.

Thirty-seven

AT THE HOSPITAL she parked near the stone stairs to the main entrance and got out of the car. For a moment she stood looking across the dry lawn at a gazebo that reminded her of many things in what seemed now to have been another lifetime.

Inside, the station nurse and the day nurse-in-training watched her coming up the stairs. She knew their names but couldn't remember them at the moment. The station nurse would know that she had permission to visit. They said a friendly "Good morning," and she said "Good morning" back to them. Walking away, she could feel them watching her in silence, maybe feeling sorry for her, and sorry about what had happened to her doctor friend, whom they'd remember from her two visits here.

In the room Kate stood for a moment until her eyes had adjusted, then she took off her coat and hung it on the hook by the bathroom door. Dark in here, with the blinds half closed. She could smell medication and the carbolic soap, and she could hear the clicking of the intravenous pump. She put on the white coat and gloves and the mask and paper hat, then she sat down on the bedside chair.

Monitors and wires and sensors. Red and green lines moving on the cardiograph. So very advanced, this place. Claire had commented on that, and had been impressed by it.

On the telephone Dr. Winters had said that the scan showed a swelling on both sides of the brain, coup and contrecoup, worse on the right side, probably from the primary impact of her head against the door post or the window. But the swellings were coming down, and because the blood-flow indicators around the cochlear nerve system were all normal it was possible that Claire could hear, if with a reduced processing capacity.

And so Kate began talking to her. She talked about the farm and the Andersons and David's history there. She said she'd seen a gazebo like the one back home in the hospital garden, no tree overhanging it, but the same wooden structure.

She sat in silence, watching these eyelids and the familiar curve of lips that never moved. She leaned close and whispered, "Claire, it's me, Kate."

She watched and waited.

She described the room she was in. A good room, she said. A safe room. Dim light through half-closed blinds, like the light of mornings and evenings, even though it was full day-light outside. She told Claire that everyone was asking about her. She spoke to Hélène every day on the telephone, and both Hélène and Mr. Chandler would be coming as soon as they were allowed to visit. Father William at the church and Mildred at the hotel had asked about her too.

She stood up from the chair and crossed to the window, where with thumb and forefinger she pried apart two slats of the wooden blind. Bare trees and yellow grass and the car park out there, and the city beyond. A few evergreens. A glimpse of the ocean, still and nearly purple in the winter light.

She stood there for a while longer, then she returned to the chair. She put on a fresh right glove and opened the Vaseline jar on the bedside table and with a tissue put a thin film of lotion on Claire's lips. There was no wastebasket and so she wrapped the tissue in another and put them in her pocket.

Then she sat back, in the coat and paper hat and mask and gloves, and waited. *Remember this*, she said to herself. *This. All of it. There is nothing to understand. Nothing. It just is.* She reached for another tissue and dried her eyes.

Through the door not far away she could hear sounds in the hallway, quick footsteps on the vinyl floor. When she heard voices outside the door, she rose from the chair and walked there. Through the pebbled glass she could see the shape of a person, then the door opened.

It was not the regular day nurse but one she'd seen before in a hallway. She stood holding a white enamel tray with medical supplies against her hip.

"And you are?" The nurse studied her.

"I'm Kate Henderson. A friend. Dr. Winters gave me permission to be here."

"Yes, she did mention that. I'm the wound nurse."

The nurse walked to the bed and turned on the lamp. It hummed and flickered and then it came on, bright and harsh. She set the tray down on the metal table, took gloves and a mask from the dispensers and put them on. At the intravenous stand she snapped a finger against one of the air traps and then picked up the chart and wrote in it.

Kate kept back and watched. After a while she said, "Can I do something? Help with anything?"

"We need to change the bandages," said the nurse. "You can help me turn her. We'll also shift her a bit. Bedsores, you know. Close your coat buttons all the way up and put on fresh everything else. Gloves, mask, and hat. Quite firmly, the hat. When you're done come to the other side of the bed."

She did as told and together they rolled Claire onto her side. She rested Claire's head on her forearm and held her with both hands while the nurse took off the bandages on Claire's temple and on her neck, inspected the wounds, and dusted a yellow powder on them.

"These two are the bad ones. They had glass splinters in

them. She could have cut an artery or broken her neck with those impacts. And there are some other bad spots that she'll feel for a while."

The nurse applied fresh bandages, settled Claire back against her pillow, and clicked off the lamp and picked up the tray. She stood as before with its edge against her hip.

"On the bright side," she said, "it could have been far worse. An impact like that. And there's no sign of an infection that I can see. I think your friend will be all right."

When the nurse had left, Kate sat on the bedside chair again and leaned close. With her gloved hand she stroked Claire's cheek and said, "You're getting better, Claire. And you're in a safe place here. You came twice to look at it. The trauma centre, you called it. It feels like a really good hospital. Very modern."

She sat a while longer in the chair, then she leaned forward again and close to Claire's ear she said, "I'm leaving now, Claire. But I'll be back. I'll probably come most days now, to see you getting better and better." She touched Claire's cheek again and said, "Bye for now. Just rest, Claire. You are in a safe place."

In the bathroom she threw the tissues into the wastebasket, then took off the white coat and the hat and mask and gloves and put them in the hamper. When she left, the door clicked shut with hardly a sound.

She walked past the nurses' station and down the echoing stairs, holding on to the rail and not seeing anything, just letting her feet do the work. Step and step and step. At the bottom she paused and told herself it was all right, and she sat down and leaned her head against the wall. She sat like this for a few deep breaths, and when she heard someone say, "Lady, you all right? You want some help?" she opened her eyes and saw a man with a broom, and she pulled herself up and said, "No, thank you, I'm fine. Thank you," and she walked away, through the lobby and through the heavy door, pushing against it with her shoulder, and out into the too-bright light of day.

She unlocked the car but then turned and walked along the gravel drive, around an empty flower bed and up the three steps to the gazebo. A wood floor in here as well. She hiked up her coat and sat down tailor-fashion. She wanted to lie down on the cold floor and go to sleep, wake up in the past, and not even that long ago a past, wake up next to Edward with her head in the crook of his arm.

She sat a while longer, then she stood up and walked back to the Fleetmaster and got in. She stepped on the starter knob and listened to the engine. There was even a radio with little pearl-and-chrome controls. She clicked it on and found a station and turned it low for company.

Then she backed the car away from the stone wall, spun the wheel hard and shifted into first, and drove off.

———

At the telephone exchange on Barrington Street, she booked a long-distance call to London. Then she sat on the little stool in the telephone booth, waiting. It was mid-afternoon by then and London was four hours ahead. She hoped Delbert was still at the Elgin, because that was the only number she had for him. Minutes later she had him on the telephone.

"Terrible," he said after he'd heard her out. "Oh my God. That's just terrible. The poor woman. And you, too. I'm so sorry to hear all that. And you say he looked like Thomas?"

"No. Not just *looked like*. I know it was him. And with every day I'm more sure of it. I know it sounds unlikely, but I swear it was that same sneer that I know so well. Those eyes."

"It's not impossible," said Delbert. "I asked at some of the other shelters and he wasn't anywhere. He could have killed you both."

"I think he meant to. It felt like it. So brutal and deliberate."

"I'll ask around some more and let you know. And you, Kate? How are you?"

She told him she was getting better. Lots of bruises and sometimes a ringing in her ears, but even that was fading. She described life on the farm in a few sentences and gave him the number there.

Two days later on the telephone Delbert told her that he was coming over.

"You are? I'm glad, Delbert. But how?"

"On a half-empty troop transport. It leaves in ten days. I'm ex-service, and it turns out that for the time being I can travel for free on a ship like that. Thomas could have gone the same way. All these ships going back and forth now in safe waters. I should be there by the end of February."

"Did you find out anything about him?"

"No. No one has seen him. I spoke to the social services woman again, and she doesn't know how Thomas found out where you are. But really, that wouldn't have been hard to do. At the hospitals Claire would have told a number of people, in case of emergencies or if her substitute needed to check something with her. Anyway. I'm coming over and I'll find him. Have the police been in touch again?"

"No. Not one word since that interview at the hospital. I'll get a map for you and I'll draw in exactly where it happened. Good. I'm glad you're coming over, Delbert."

Thirty-eight

NOW SHE DROVE INTO THE CITY every day to sit with Claire. Sometimes Hélène and Mr. Chandler were there as well, on the other side of the bed, also shrouded in white coats, hats, gloves, and masks. They were staying at a hotel on the harbourfront.

And shortly before noon one day, while Kate was there alone, Claire woke to consciousness. She woke quickly and almost without transition, like a sleeper being startled awake by something. She opened her eyes and said, "Kate . . ."

She moved and tried to sit up, but then groaned with pain and lay back again and closed her eyes. "What's going on, Kate?"

Kate reached for her hand and told her what had happened.

"I had a dream," said Claire. "Just now, I think. I was in a garden full of flowers, and little birds with long beaks were sipping from them. Hummingbirds, making tiny sounds. Everything so peaceful. A little paradise, and a high garden wall to keep it safe."

"And you are safe now, Claire."

A nurse came and checked Claire's vitals, and then Dr. Winters came as well. She was smiling. "Welcome back, Dr. Giroux. How do you feel?"

Nine days later, after a final scan that showed that the swellings had come down completely, Dr. Winters discharged Claire into Kate's care for full recovery.

"No excitement," said Dr. Winters. "Nothing strenuous, no bending down, no loud noises, no bright lights. Just good food and rest and a bit of walking a few times a day. Keep the gauze on the wounds for now, and after a few more days even that can go. Dr. Giroux can make that decision. To pull the stitches she can come in, or you can do it for her. But any changes, call me right away."

The day she took Claire to the farm was a Saturday in late February. Hélène and Mr. Chandler were at the hospital, and they all helped Claire down the stairs one sideways step at a time and into the back seat of the Fleetmaster.

Hélène reached and gave Claire the gentlest of hugs.

"I would have loved to come along, my dear, but the doctor said better not. And she's probably right. The less commotion, the better. We'll come up soon and visit. You let me know when."

Driving north to the horse farm now. The closest thing to home in this faraway land. Hardly any traffic. A flock of ravens flying low and swooping up in front of the car. A cold day, but the car had a good heater. She arranged the rear-view mirror to see Claire in the back seat in the light from the side windows. Sitting with her eyes closed. Pale, thin, exhausted.

The wound under the gauze on her temple had been large, but it was healed. A great ragged area of hair clipped off, and on the side of her neck, the gash with stitches in it still. And painful contusions all over her body.

Claire opened her eyes and saw her in the mirror.

"When will Delbert be here, Kate?"

"By the end of February, he said. So maybe just another week or so. His ship will have left by now."

"Good. I like that man."

At the farm, she pulled up at the entrance to the main building. The Andersons came to help, and Tippy came out of her doghouse and stretched and yawned.

Mrs. Anderson put an arm around Claire's waist and held her up, and they walked her into the house, where the spare room had been made ready. A calm light in the room. Dark walls with paintings on them, bookshelves, and area rugs on the wood floor. The hospital bed near the window, and a few chairs and a desk. A wood-fired iron stove in the corner, giving off heat.

Kate helped Claire undress and put on a nightgown and crawl into bed.

"Anything you need or want, Claire. Right? During the day there's this little hand bell on the side table. See it? At night, just push this button and I'll be here in a minute."

The little button communicated with a bell in the groom's bunk room. She'd suggested it and bought the supplies at the general store, and Mr. Anderson had strung a thin temporary wire and installed everything.

The cowboys for the wild-herd roundup had arrived and had moved into the bunkhouse on the other side of the yard. Three men, in their late twenties perhaps, lean and weathered in jeans and scuffed boots. Their calls and laughter brought new life to the farm.

Mr. Anderson said that they'd cut out three horses from the wild herd already, with four more to come.

Kate cranked up Claire's bed and pulled up a chair. Out the window they could see a paddock with three horses and three men in it, the horses bunching into a corner to get away from the men.

"Do you want to watch a bit?" asked Kate. "Those are wild horses in the early stage of being tamed. Side-roping, it's called. I've heard about it but I've never seen it done."

"So let's watch."

In the paddock one of the cowboys was swinging a loop while another was moving in on the horses along the rail. The moment the first one bolted, the cowboy with the rope let fly the loop. It caught the forefoot of the bolting horse, and he yanked at the rope. The horse tripped and fell hard to the ground, and immediately all three cowboys were on top of it.

"The poor horse," said Claire. "What are they doing?"

"They're not hurting it. They're just putting on a special headstall and then . . . look, they're tying side ropes to the hind legs and attaching them to the headstall to restrict the horse's movement."

The men leapt away, and the horse struggled up and stood still for a moment. Then it kicked out both hind legs hard. Instantly the side ropes yanked its head down, and the horse stumbled and nearly fell. It kicked out one leg, and the side rope yanked its head hard sideways. It stood still and blew and looked down at its feet. It took a few careful steps and the side ropes were just long enough to allow that. Then it stood and kicked both hind legs again, and this time it fell down hard. It struggled up again and just stood, unsure what to do next.

One of the men was already swinging a fresh loop and another was moving in on the other two horses. One horse broke and the loop caught its foreleg, and the horse tripped and fell with a thump and instantly again the three men were on top of it.

"And then what?" said Claire. "When they're all roped up?"

"Patience, mostly. Eventually the horses will allow the men to approach them. At some point the side ropes come off, and if the horse goes wild again, the process is repeated. Eventually the horses accept the men and allow themselves to be touched. Then comes accepting the saddle, and finally accepting the rider in the saddle. It all takes a while. Weeks of constant work, David told me once."

In her nights in the barn, in the protective dark around her, the horses in their stalls became her friends. So did the stars, and sometimes glimpses of the moon in the cracks in the barn walls.

Eddie, where are you? So thrilled, so in love with what you are doing. With your plans for your career. Consumed by it all.

She could feel that in her heart in the nights, feel it all the way across two thousand miles in the dark and be sad and angry with him for having been so distracted during that one brief telephone conversation. For being so careless about keeping in touch.

On her cot, in her nest under the blankets, she wore an old track suit from a closet in David's room, along with a wool toque and hockey socks either from him or from the Andersons' son. The little bell was mounted on the wall next to the cot, and her boots stood next to the cot, in just the right spot for her feet to find them quickly.

She could hear the horses even in her sleep, and loved it. She felt sorry for the fresh-caught wild ones, roped up and away from their friends and families, in this alien and surely terrifying environment.

Often before she went to visit them, she'd climb into the hay bins and sweep the corners with her bare hands to collect hayseeds. Then, standing at their stalls and reaching out, she'd whisper to them and see them freeze at first but then relax and inch closer. One night, one of the two that were without ropes already and were ready for saddle training took hayseeds from her cupped hands. She felt privileged, and she searched for a name for that horse. A white marking on its forehead, right between the eyes. Not long enough to be a stripe or a blaze, but a star!

"*Starling*," she said to the horse as it stood chewing seeds and taking more with tongue and lips. "Starling, that's you. Come get it all. Enjoy."

Thirty-nine

ONE DAY SHE HAD JUST brought Claire tea on a tray when she heard a taxi. She looked out the window and saw Delbert pulling a duffel bag off the back seat and slinging the strap over his shoulder.

"I'll go and talk to him," she said to Claire. "Want me to bring him in?"

"Of course. No, wait! Do I look a mess?"

"No, you don't. You are a patient in bed, but you've got some colour today. You're getting better, Claire."

"All right then."

Kate went outside and talked to Delbert and then led the way inside. "Don't be shocked when you see her," she told him. "It was brutal on her. She's much thinner, and she's still weak. But she's eating regular meals now, and we go for walks two, three times a day. She's on the mend."

Kate took him to Claire's room and said, "Look who's here," and she waved him into the room.

For a moment she stood listening at the door. "Dr. Giroux," she heard him say. "This is just—I am so very sorry for what happened to you. And I feel twice as bad because I thought I'd made my point with him . . ."

And Kate walked away.

The Andersons put him up in David's room, and Kate visited him there. She told him about the creaking in the night, but Delbert said he didn't care.

In the morning after breakfast she showed him to the station wagon. She gave him the keys, unfolded the map on the bonnet, and pointed at the places she'd marked for him.

"Saint Homais, here. It's where Claire's mother lives. Thomas knew where that is because he's been there, early on. And this is where he ran into us. Right here."

Delbert looked closely at the spots, then he refolded the map to show the target area and tossed it onto the passenger seat.

"It may take me a few days. If I don't come back in the evenings, I'll call you. All right?"

"All right."

He looked over his shoulder at the main house. "That poor woman. So brave, and so badly hurt. Outside and in. You can tell. She doesn't say how she feels about it, and she doesn't have to. It's deep. For a man she was trying to help to show her such contempt."

Kate watched as Delbert slid into the seat and put the gear lever into neutral. He stepped on the starter. Then he pulled shut the door and cranked down the window.

"Be careful," she said to him.

He nodded but didn't say another word. He backed the car out of the shed, gave a little wave, and drove off.

Forty

HE WAS GONE for three days while Kate spent time with Claire, walked and did stretch-and-strength exercises with her. Once she rode out with the cowboys. They were cutting out more horses from the wild herd and bringing them to the training paddock. The first three were in another area by now. One of them, not Starling, had gone wild again and had to be put back into side ropes. The other two nuzzled it and nickered to it, and the roped horse moved in baby steps and seemed to be looking after them longingly.

Delbert called every evening, as he'd said he would. His last phone call came from Annapolis Royal; he didn't say why he was there, only that he was on his way to the farm but he'd be arriving late.

When she heard the station wagon drive into the yard, she stepped into the boots and went to meet him. He came her way limping badly across the yard, and in the light from the bulb above the barn door she could see that there was blood on his trousers.

"What happened?" she said as she helped him up to his room. "What happened to your leg?"

"I'll show you." He put a brown paper bag on the table and grimaced with pain as he lowered himself onto the side of the bed. "Damn. That hurts. Shouldn't have sat down. Might not be able to get up again. Can you please undo my shoes?"

He leaned back on his elbows while she took off his shoes, then unbuckled his belt. "Arch up a bit," she told him. "So I can pull off your trousers."

There was a blood-soaked bandage wrapped around his right thigh.

"What happened?"

"A pitchfork. He got me with a pitchfork. Right through, in and out. Long, sharp tines on those things. I'll tell you, but can we do this first? The doctor said to clean it again with alcohol, then another needle, half in the muscle near the entry wound and half near the exit. Then a fresh bandage. It's all in the paper bag."

"What kind of needle?"

"Penicillin. The doctor was a good man. He gave me a tetanus shot and offered to put me up for the night, but I explained that I had to move on."

"What doctor? Where?"

"I can't remember. In a town on the way here."

"All right. Hold still now." She took off the bandage and looked at his thigh. A puncture wound all the way through the lateral quadriceps.

"Was the fork dirty?"

"I think it was used for hay, not mucking out, if that's what you mean."

"Hay on the ground can be bad enough, but the tetanus shot should cover that." She cleaned both entry and exit with alcohol, drew penicillin from the small bottle, and injected half of it an inch away from each wound, at a slight angle towards the wound path. Then she put on fresh patches of gauze, wrapped a length of bandage around his thigh, and fixed it there with two safety pins through the end of the fabric.

She stood up. "All done. Now tell me what happened."

But he didn't tell her that night. He couldn't. He lay back on the bed with his feet still on the floor. Exhausted, and with the penicillin and the attention to his injury he seemed calm and already half asleep.

She knelt on the bed, got her arms under him, and lifted and yanked and dragged him, straightened him out so that his head came to rest on the pillow. Then she covered him with the duvet.

"Good night," she said to his closed eyes. He did not stir. She watched him a moment longer, then she turned out the light and left.

———

In the morning she went to look for him but he wasn't in his room. He was outside already, in the station wagon, rubbing at spots with a rag.

"Hey, easy, easy!" she said to him. "Go easy on your leg. Bedrest for a day would be good. Give that muscle a chance to recover. What are you doing?"

"Wiping up blood. Mostly his, but mine too. Good thing these seats are oilcloth."

"Where is he now?"

"In the hospital."

"What happened?"

He looked at her, then he put down the rag and limped around to the rear of the car. The tailgate stood open, and he sat down on one side of the small loading platform, grimacing as he moved his bad leg. He patted the platform by his side, and she sat down.

"It took me a full two days to find him, Kate, but I'll give you the short version."

"Well, not too short. A few details too."

"You want details? All right . . . So I knew there'd have to be paint and some damage from the impact at the front of his lorry, and he'd need to have it fixed or hide it somewhere. In the end, after I'd searched body shops and garages for that kind of evidence, and for him, it was the tire tracks that gave him away. Very different from tractors or other farm vehicles. These tracks were going to a barn in a field not far from where he crashed into you. I'd seen them before, and yesterday late in the day I went back there to look inside the barn.

"I was careful, but even so he must have seen me or heard me, because the moment I was inside he came at me with that pitchfork. It was dark in there and at first I could hardly see him, but I managed to back away and grab a bin rail, a good solid stick about five and a half feet long. He'd gotten me in the leg with the first run, but with that stick now I could hold him off. Not for long though, I knew that, before my leg would stiffen. And him all the while taking runs at me. A dangerous thing, a pitchfork. He looked at my stick and grinned.

"We circled each other and I told him what he'd done to you and Dr. Giroux, but he only laughed. He knew he had me. He with a pitchfork and I with just a stick, and injured already.

"It's in his eyes, Kate. This time I could see it, even in the bad light in the barn. In his eyes and all over his face, the mean craziness, and when it came over him the men in his platoon would have seen it too. Anyway. He would have killed me. I knew it then and I still know it now. He was taking hard runs at me, stabbing, stabbing with forward knee-bends like some medieval lancer, but then I found an up-and-outward move to stop and deflect the fork and then to free my stick. On the return I could put my whole body into a full swing, and that's when things started to change.

"I had warned him, Kate. Back home, when I talked to him. Warned him what would happen if he ever harmed either of you again. Obviously he wasn't listening, and so this time I showed him. I did, Kate. If you want to know, I broke both his legs, one at the knee, and I broke his right arm on the pitchfork. I could hear and feel the bones crack and give way, and then as he went down I got him on the head too."

He looked at her sideways. "That's what the blood in the car is from. And from my leg."

"What happened then? Is he alive?"

"I don't know about *now*, but the last time I saw him he was still breathing. I managed to drag him into the back seat and then I drove to the hospital in Annapolis Royal. It was night by then but I'd seen the hospital during the day. Anyway, I dumped him at the entrance, rang the emergency bell, and drove off before anyone could see me and ask questions. I was bleeding quite a bit myself, and on the way home I saw the lit sign for an all-night pharmacy, and the chemist gave me directions to the doctor."

She said nothing for a while. Sitting next to him on the metal lip of the trunk. Then she said, "Do you think he'll live?"

"I don't know. He was alive when I left him there. Within an inch, I'd say."

"You'll have to tell Claire."

"I know. How? The way I told you?"

"More or less. Maybe more about how he came at you first, so you had no choice."

Kate was in the room when Delbert told Claire. He stood at the foot of the bed, talking, and Claire listened and asked no questions. Not one. When Delbert had finished she lay back and closed her eyes. Dim winter light in the room and a deep silence.

"It's all right, Delbert," Claire said eventually. "Thank you for telling me."

For another long moment it was very still in the room. Then Claire said, "Maybe go now, both of you. Please."

Later that day it was Kate who took the call when the police rang to tell her that an Englishman with the name she'd given them had been found at a hospital and identified from some papers in his wallet. He was badly injured, with multiple fractures and a cranial injury. He was unconscious, but he was expected to live. She asked the policeman to hold and then she unplugged the telephone, carried it into Claire's room, and plugged it in there. The policeman was still on the line and she told him that she'd be passing the receiver to Dr. Giroux.

Claire took the receiver. She lay back against her pillows. She was very pale.

"Yes?" she said.

Kate stepped back and walked to the window and put her forehead to the cold glass. Snowing now. Small flakes on a northerly, the prevailing wind here. Ravens in the tops of the pine trees by the farm entrance, large black birds cawing raucously and lifting off only to circle once and then to come back and settle again on branches that bent under their weight.

Suddenly, more firmly and in a stronger voice, as though she'd made up her mind about something, Claire was saying, "Yes, officer. I do understand that. It seems reasonable." There was a silence as she listened, then she said, "No, I will not pursue it. But thank you for letting us know."

Forty-one

THAT NIGHT Mr. Anderson came running to the barn. Kate heard him call her name, and she had her feet over the side of the cot and in the boots even before he'd opened the man door. He stood in the brighter rectangle of it and said, "Kate! It's your friend Edward on the phone from Calgary."

She followed him quickly inside. The telephone was back in the hall and the receiver lay on the sideboard next to it. She picked it up.

"Eddie, is that really you?"

"It is, Katie. Sorry, I know it's later where you are, and I'm sorry I didn't keep in touch but I couldn't really—"

"Couldn't?" she interrupted him. "Eddie! Do you know how long it's been? And all this time you couldn't find a telephone somewhere and a moment to call?"

"I know, I know. But I've been away, flying, and it's all going so well. I'm sorry, I know, but listen, I just found out and I wanted to tell you. In two days I'll be at the Greenwood base in Nova Scotia and we can see each other."

"Greenwood," she said. "I've seen road signs for that. It's not very far from here. I have so much to tell you."

"All good?"

"No, but in the end, for now, yes. Claire and I were in an accident, and guess who caused it."

She told him the full story, and he listened without interruption.

"How terrible," he said when she'd finished. "But at least you are all getting better. Uncle Delbert too?"

"Yes, he too. It's good to have him here. He's still limping a bit, but he's a good healer. He'll be fine. About Thomas, the police told Claire that they can't find the truck, and that because of the timing his injuries are obviously from some other accident. In any case, without the truck they don't have any evidence that it was Thomas who ran into us. They asked her if she wished to pursue the case, and she said no. She wants to have nothing more to do with him. I hope he just disappears and we'll never see him again."

"Yes, let's hope so. Katie, get a piece of paper and a pen and I'll give you a number at the base. I can't wait to see you. You can stay at a hotel in town and I'll get an overnight pass or two. Or three. Are you feeling all right now?"

"Yes, I'm fine. We were both very lucky. Claire is making progress too. We pulled the stitches on her neck, and there was never any infection. Not with Delbert either. But all this will keep, Eddie . . . You should have called me, you know."

Two days later she packed her bag and said goodbye to Claire and to Delbert and the Andersons. Claire walked with her to the Fleetmaster.

"You see," she said. "I can walk on my own now, without holding on to you. I'm getting stronger, Kate."

"Yes you are, and I'm happy for you. Walk a bit every day while I'm gone, and do the exercises."

At the car Kate put her bag in the back seat and closed the door. She said, "I'm sorry I'll miss Hélène and Mr. Chandler when they come out tomorrow. I hope they'll understand, but I really want to see Edward and I don't know how long he'll be in Greenwood."

"They'll understand," said Claire. "All this has been a most unusual ordeal for us. But I think it's over now. And the trauma centre is wonderful and modern and all that, but I want to go home. I know that now, Kate."

"I've been thinking that too, that I'm ready to go home. But first I want to talk to Edward about our plans."

"Of course." Claire gave her a hug. "Drive carefully, and if you stay longer than three nights, give me a call. Or give me a call anyway. During the days."

"I will." She climbed in, started the engine, and backed out of the shed. Driving away she cranked down the window and waved. Claire waved back with both arms.

A blue sky today, warmer and not so windy. Soon she could see the ocean to her right. Emerald-green and vast, and to her left a landscape of dry grass and great boulders rounded and white with age. The ocean stayed with her for a long time, until she turned south towards the Annapolis Valley.

Forty-two

HE WAS IN UNIFORM. From behind, and from the side as well, he looked so different. Thinner and a bit taller-looking even. Standing very erect at the front desk with his cap under his left arm. She heard the clerk call him sir, then the clerk noticed her sneaking up on Edward to surprise him, and he raised an eyebrow.

Edward turned and saw her. He shouted, "*Katie!*" and he dropped his cap and lifted her up and swung her round. Over his shoulder she saw people in the hotel lobby going by in a full giddy circle, looking on and smiling. By the time Edward put her down and hugged her close and kissed her, she had already forgiven him absolutely everything.

The first two nights were much like their night at the London hotel had been. Laughter and pillow fights; undressing feverishly and making love all over the bed as wide as a beach.

Luxurious baths and dinners by candlelight, and talking about their various adventures over the past few months. Holding hands.

During the days she walked the town, spent time on the telephone with Claire and with Hélène and Delbert, and sat on a cold iron bench at the fence by the end of the runways, watching airplanes take off and land.

The third and last night was different. It began at dinner when she asked him about his plans for the future. And were his plans still *their* plans as they had talked about them, however vaguely, in England?

"Of course," he said. "But . . ."

She caught him looking at the ring on her finger, and she left her hand where it was, on the white tablecloth next to her plate.

"But what?"

"Katie, look at me. At my uniform. What's still missing? Can you tell me?"

She looked at him across the candle flame and wished she knew what he was talking about, but she didn't.

"What, Eddie?"

"My wings, of course! It's a badge half as big as my hand and it goes here." He touched his left shoulder. "There are so many more things I need to do. Courses to take, hours to fly, exams to pass, some of them hard as hell. I don't really know how long it'll take, but I know now that I can do it. It's been difficult, but I stuck it out and now I'm so close. And they're giving me this chance. Good people, Katie. Strong but fair leadership. When they left Britain they could have just left me behind."

"But they didn't leave you behind."

"No, they didn't, but before we took off for Winnipeg I had to sign an application for Canadian citizenship. So I could continue taking their training and their money. They were good to me. This is an RCAF uniform, Katie." He ran his hand over the front of his tunic. "The C stands for Canadian."

"So? What are you saying?"

"That I want my wings."

"More than anything else. I know that. But does that mean you'll have to stay in Canada? Will we have to live here?"

"Maybe. Maybe not. We have bases in Britain, and now with the occupation we also have bases in Germany, France, Italy, the Middle East, you name it. Even in Africa. We are allies and that means a lot in the military. It's like a brotherhood, and it's exciting and it feels good. So that's what I'm focusing on for now."

"And you and I?"

"There's no change there. I love you as much as ever, but exactly what or when or how—we'll see that more clearly in a while. There is talk of Egypt next."

"Egypt! And then what? When and how long, Eddie? What's a *while*? Claire wants to go home, and Delbert does too, I'm sure. I have some decisions to make."

"Decisions?"

"Yes, depending on our plans."

He looked at her strangely. "Our plans," he said. "Katie . . . I'm not ready to nail down anything just yet. I can't. It's all their agenda, not mine."

He looked upset suddenly. He said the only thing he knew for sure at this point was that he wanted his wings. A career as a military pilot. It was demanding, and even more so for him because he hadn't gone to the academy. But he was getting close. And so that was what he was focusing on.

That night up in their room was different. No pillow fights, no laughter. They made love once in the night and once in the morning with the first pale light in the room. That last one made her cry. She knew that in a way it all depended on how she saw things. Interesting plans of her own would help; a purpose independent of him, which she'd had until recently. And so this was all new and it was sudden.

When he traced her tears with his finger she thought he must know all that and perhaps feel it too. He looked guilty and so she hugged him closer. It was not his fault.

He said nothing. But what useful thing was there to say?

Forty-three

LATER THAT SAME DAY she drove back to the horse farm. The ocean to her left now, the stretches of dry grass and boulders to her right. She saw foxes, saw an eagle in a tall white pine not far from the road. But it was a different road now, a different ocean and different boulders. A different noontime sun shining down onto her hands on the steering wheel. The ring still there, but some other meaning to it now.

At the farm Claire studied her face and did not probe. But at one point when they were alone in the living room she finally did ask how it had gone, and Kate told her. Claire listened. She nodded and after a while she said, "It's complicated. Do you want to talk about it?"

"In time. Not now. I need to work it out for myself first."

Claire said she understood.

In the night she tried to see the ring in the dark and could not. But she could see the stars and part of the moon between the boards in the wall, and she could hear the horses snuffling and stirring, and she loved them. She loved this cot, too. No over-large bed this, but her very own snug space to support and contain her. In it she could stretch out and close her eyes and listen, and think and feel, and as she did so, her sadness seemed to lift gradually and a mood of acceptance and resolve to appear.

She climbed off the cot, stepped into the boots, and collected hayseed and offered it to the horses on her flat hand. Some took it, others did not. Starling did. "Good girl," Kate said to her. "Have it all. Enjoy!"

In the afternoon she and Claire took Tippy for a walk, and they sat in the dry grass by the eastern fence. It was a sunny day, but the wind came again out of the north, from a long fetch across the ocean, and it was cold. They wore wool skirts and coats and wool hats.

Kate reached and turned up Claire's collar over the injury. It was healed, but for a long time yet warmth would still be better for it than cold. They hugged their knees. Not far away a wild horse emerged from behind a bush and saw them. It froze, then it leapt up on all four feet at once, spun around, and galloped away. Tippy lifted her nose and sniffed, then she rested her head on her paws again.

"Kate," said Claire after a while. "Like I said the other day, I'm ready to go home. I almost feel like that horse just now. Up and away. I almost can't wait. What about you?"

Kate said she was thinking about it. She asked Claire how she might be travelling back.

"Delbert has found a British HMS Something, and the ship's doctor can't go. If I sign on in his place for the trip we can all travel for free. The three of us. Come along, Kate."

"Delbert and you?" She rearranged herself so she could see Claire without turning her head. "Claire?"

And Claire coloured a bit. "No, it's nothing like that. Not really. Or maybe it is. I do like him. There's something very good about him, Kate. And solid and kind. I think you know that too."

"Yes, I do know that. I've known that all along. Ever since he taught me self-defence and gave me all those gun runs. Most of the money I have is because he gave me the opportunity to earn it."

"His leg is much better and he wants to go back too," said Claire. "And you, Kate? What about Edward now? Can I ask?"

"Yes, you can. And the truth is I don't know. I haven't heard from him since Greenwood. I think he's back in Winnipeg. I feel like it's all up in the air now, and that's really my fault because I left myself wide open for it."

"Maybe. But don't be too hard on yourself over it. Sometimes it's good to step back a bit and see how things develop naturally, without forcing them. What about your own plans? What is it that *you* want? Are you thinking about staying? If so, for how long? Do you feel you fit in here?"

"Do I fit in here."

"Without me and Delbert."

"I'd miss you a lot. And do what here? Sit and wait for Edward? I don't think so."

Kate shifted around again, this time to look out through the fence to the trees where the wild horse had disappeared.

"And you, Claire? Are you finally finished with Thomas?"

"Yes, I am. I was already mostly finished with him when I divorced him. And now, after this last thing, I have made peace with my sense of obligation, and I don't care anymore where he is or how he is. I'll have nothing more to do with him. I just want to go home and get back to work."

For a while they sat in silence. Then Kate said, "I need a bit of time. When is that ship leaving?"

"Soon, actually. In less than a week."

In dreams that night two men in long coats and hats had broken into the secret room. They took down the chapter cards and read them with large magnifying glasses, looking for details. They ripped up the floor and found the manuscript. Then they sat going through page after page with their magnifying glasses, looking behind the words and for words between the lines. They were skilled searchers taking their time, and she knew that in the end they would find whatever secrets David had hidden in the manuscript.

She woke with a start and sat up on the cot. Gripped the canvas-covered side rails and looked around.

"David," she said. And louder. "*David?*"

But of course he was not there. Pale light in the cracks in the wall. A new day dawning.

After breakfast she sat a while longer with the Andersons and told them she'd be leaving with Claire and Delbert. She thanked them for her time on the farm, but she had a feeling now that David might perhaps not be coming home so soon, and that there was something she needed to do in England.

They looked at her and waited a bit, then Mrs. Anderson said, "Well, if you have to go . . . We loved having you here, you know that. The three of you."

Mrs. Anderson stood up and came around the table and gave her a hug. And Mr. Anderson, once he saw how much the women were moved by this turn of events, stood up too from his chair and he gave Kate a big hug as well . . .

On the journey home, her and Claire's favourite spot on the ship was again the foredeck, where they often stood holding on to the rail, facing the salt breeze and grinning into it and at each other. Sometimes Delbert joined them.

They saw whales blowing, saw icebergs and saw ships going in the other direction. They waved at them, but the ships were always too far away to see if anyone waved back.

Two weeks later they were back in England, watching from deck as hawsers were made fast and the gangway was rolled into place. The last week of April already, and a sweet smell of home in the air.

ENGLAND
～ MAY 1946 ～

Forty-four

EARLY ON IN THEIR TIME TOGETHER Claire had shown Kate one of her favourite spots in Talbot: the graves of three Roman soldiers hidden in an overgrown, elevated corner of the cemetery. Men dead nearly two thousand years but their names and dates still legible in the marble. Their military ranks even, by the number of short Roman swords chiselled into stone. She'd parted the bushes for Kate like revealing a secret, and then had shown her the best grave marker, from the top of which one could see far across the trees towards the roofs of Sidcup and further away to the river Thames and the city of London, defiant in the war, with windows flashing copper in the morning sun. Westminster and Big Ben and the Houses of Parliament; monuments to tradition. Far away, and not so far. A bird could fly there in minutes.

Kate had loved it. London and surrounds all there before her, vast and etched, the sky turning from copper to gold; steel-blue

KURT PALKA

behind the buildings as yet but the light beginning to warm there as well.

Now, on the Sunday after they were back from Canada, Claire and Kate visited the cemetery to put flowers on the graves of their loved ones: Claire's baby William, Kate's mother, her father, and her aunt Catrina.

On their way out of the cemetery Kate said she wanted to stand on the Roman grave marker once more, and so they walked to it and Claire helped her up. She helped Kate place her feet securely, and then she held on to Kate's knees to steady her. And while Kate looked out and called out what there was to be seen in the play of light on it all, Claire had a moment of profound insight, and for that moment she was filled with a great sense of wonder and relief at the possibility that, horrific or beautiful, all was exactly as it was meant to be.

The next day Claire dove into her busy working life like a swimmer into water, but Kate took her re-entry more slowly. What she would have to do required the final acceptance of a loss long denied, and it could not be rushed.

She visited the secret room, and everything in it was as it had been before the trip to Canada: the manuscript and her knot in the string around it; the pistol and the corkboard with his chapter cards and her notes to him. Even the maple leaf that she'd pinned to the board a year and a half ago. Fresh and golden-red at the time, a gift literally from on high.

She locked up again and walked to the tea room. Tony was pleased to see her, and he showed her his latest acquisition: a large, shiny record-playing machine that he'd found at an army surplus store. The machine operated on halfpenny slugs that he sold at the counter.

She bought a dozen slugs and then sat there with her mug of Horlicks and listened to Vera Lynn and Gracie Fields and Ella Fitzgerald and Jo Stafford until somehow and from somewhere among these women's voices and their words, she found the resolve to do what she'd promised.

In front of the building she looked over her shoulder once more before inserting the key, then she was in the hallway. *Shhh . . . quietly, quietly.* She turned the key and turned the doorknob to the secret room. Stepped inside, closed the door behind her, and set the shopping bag next to the typewriter on the desk.

She stood and looked around; the same room, and yet somehow, because of her mission here today, a changed room already.

She took the letter opener, knelt, and lifted out the sections of floorboards. There. She set manuscript and gun on the desk and put the floorboards back.

Minutes later she stood in the little concrete courtyard, crumpling the first three or four pages like he'd said. She dropped them into the barrel and poured coal oil over them. Struck a match and dropped it in. Slow blue flames spreading. She crumpled more pages and fed the fire with them. One page at a time. Good flames now, almost no smoke. More pages, and more, methodically, page after crumpled page. She felt the heat of the fire on her face, saw the air shimmer above the barrel. More pages. The pages in Russian, and the one with the translation. It took her almost an hour to burn the entire manuscript. Then the chapter cards. She unpinned them, stacked them in small piles on the desk, and pushed the pins back into the corkboard. She made certain that the filing cabinet and the desk drawers were in fact empty, then she carried the cards outside, crumpled them up, and poured coal oil over them. Dropped in the match. They burned more slowly, but they too disappeared, stack by little stack. And finally her letters to him, all of them.

In the end she looked down into the barrel and stirred the ashes, broke them up with a stick she'd found on the ground. Stirred and stirred.

She cleaned up in the WC in the hallway. Soot and coal oil on her hands. Smudges of soot on her face too. She rinsed her face and scrubbed face and hands with the towel. Then she put the pistol in her handbag, locked up, and left.

———

She met Delbert in their usual place at the back of his building on Elgin Street. Bushes and trees in springtime leaf now, all fresh and green. A fine day. Delbert came out the door wearing a vested suit with a white shirt and tie.

"Nice outfit," she said. "What's the occasion?"

"The final job interview. Things are changing, Kate. In a few days I may be an engineer again, working for the city. I hope I can still do it."

"Of course you can."

"Put my rough ways behind me?"

"Not completely, I hope."

He grinned at her. "About the Beretta—it's the same buyer at the same address. Same iron door, same two knocks. When I called him I said three hundred and he was a bit shocked, so I let him bargain me down to two seventy. He really wants it. He deals with informed collectors, and it's an absolutely rare piece in mint condition. Highly desirable. But he wants to see it first."

Delbert handed her a piece of paper. "In case you've forgotten where it is. He'll probably try to bargain some more. Don't go any lower than two fifty. All right?"

Forty-five

AT THREE O'CLOCK IN THE MORNING she and Claire sat in the kitchen, eating a meal. Tea and sliced rye bread. Sliced tomatoes and peppers and cold cuts she'd brought home. She told Claire that while she'd been at the shop, Barbie's mother had come in.

"Remember her?" Kate said. "She lost her job at the bomb factory when they were replacing so many of us with demobbed soldiers. Well, apparently things are changing again. It's either that there are more jobs or that some of the men didn't work out. Now she has a welding job in a tractor factory."

"I've heard about those changes too," said Claire. "It'll be hard for a while longer with the rationing, but at least the economy is picking up and we're making things other than bombs and guns again."

"I suppose so. Speaking of guns, I sold the pistol today. For two hundred and fifty pounds, more than four times what it cost me. Delbert set it up. I saw him, looking very spiffy. I think his gun-running days are over, and so I suppose are mine. Edward will be relieved to hear it."

"Edward, yes. Have you heard from him?"

"No. I called the number in Winnipeg and they said he was in Newfoundland. They gave me a number but all I could do was leave a message."

"He must be in the final stretch for his wings by now."

"Probably."

Claire looked at her and waited. Then, and untypically for her who hardly ever probed, she said, "*And,* Kate? Can I ask how you are doing with it?"

Kate took her time with the answer. She cut a tomato slice in half and put it on a corner of her toast. She looked up and said, "I found some space around it, Claire. And I filled that space with my own plans. With what I want to do and *will* do for myself. Now I feel much calmer about him."

"Good. Congratulations."

"And there's something else. A big step, Claire. I finally did what I promised David to do, and I burned every last piece of paper in his room. Everything."

"Did you? So the manuscript is all gone?"

"All gone. The Russian pages, the chapter cards, everything. Maybe tell Patrick he can stop looking for it. He might be relieved to hear it."

"Tell Patrick. Interesting idea. That's quite a development, and he was good enough to tell us about fishermen and David's assignment in Russia."

"He was that. So feel free to tell him my truth as well, Claire. You were the one he was straight with. He never was with me, but one day I'd like to be able to trust that man. If only because he's my last remaining link to my family."

In the afternoon Claire drove to Riverdale Hospital. She parked in her assigned spot, walked across the car park, and entered by the side entrance. In her office she looked at the case log, then closed the door and dialled his number. Four hours earlier there. Another man answered, but a moment later Patrick was on the telephone.

"Claire! It's so good to hear your voice. I heard about the accident but I didn't know where to reach you. Where are you, and how are you feeling? How is Kate?"

She told him they were both back in England and they were fine. She was tiring more quickly than before the accident, but hopefully that too would pass. Then she told him at length about Kate's promise to David and about burning the manuscript.

He listened to her without interruption, then he said, "Wow. Let me catch my breath. Amazing. What exactly did she burn?"

Claire told him.

"*Four hundred pages?*" he said. "And pages in Russian? Cyrillic handwriting? Are you sure? Other languages use the Cyrillic alphabet as well."

"I know that, but it was Russian. We had some of it translated and it was what I'd call a descriptive detail. A person at a certain location."

"And names? Do you remember any names?"

In her run of honesty she almost said *Yes, Anna Ketov,* but she stopped herself in time and said, "No, I don't."

"And now all that is burnt, all gone? Every last page? Manuscript, chapter cards, everything?"

"Yes. Everything."

"Where did he keep the manuscript?"

"You don't need to know that, Patrick. But it's definitely gone."

"Fair enough. But why did Kate burn it all *now*? David's been gone for a year and a half."

"Because she had a certain dream."

"A dream."

"Yes. And she acted on it."

"Do you believe her, Claire?"

"Absolutely."

"And you believe in dreams?"

"Yes, I do. I learned about them in Dr. Elliott's class. Dreams matter. They are about our subconscious rubbing our noses in something we don't want to see."

"What was the dream about?"

"You can ask her that yourself one day. When you've made up with her. Which I hope will be soon. You lied to her from the beginning, trying to weasel information about that manuscript out of her, and she suspected it all along. So of course she didn't trust you."

"And so she lied back. Right? But I can understand that. She had to, because of her promise to David. And as to what you call my weaseling—remember my profession, Claire. I take it seriously. There is a certain code to it, as I'm sure there is to your profession. Certain things that we must do, and others that we absolutely must *not* do, even if there's a conflict. Anyway— so it's all gone? All his records?"

"Yes."

There was a pause, then he said, "Forgive me for asking you once more, but this is very important. Are you absolutely certain that all those papers have been destroyed? Do you trust Kate completely?"

"Yes, and yes, Patrick. I trust Kate completely."

"All right."

It was not in his short two words but in the space around them that he suddenly sounded different. Relieved, she thought. Lighter.

"What's going on, Patrick? Did you—"

"Stop, Claire! Just stop. It may not work, but I think I can find something to trade with. I can try. We're former allies, and we still share intelligence. It's all right."

"What is?"

"All of it. Let me think. I remember your house from the birthday party. Do you and Kate still live there?"

"Yes. Why?"

"It may take a couple of weeks, but for the next little while, would you mind leaving a key under the mat?"

"Why? And why do I have to ask *why* all the time. You are being very mysterious, Patrick. Is that part of your code too? Why the key under the mat?"

"Because it's cold out. At least over here it still is. Just do it, Claire."

Forty-six

THE NEW AREA SUPERVISOR at Paramedics was a young man close to Kate in age. The sign on his desk said Matt Williams, and he told her that he'd served as a medic during the war in Europe and that in the last few months he'd worked in a field hospital in France. He asked her to wait while he looked for her file in a steel cabinet. He found it and then sat reading it.

He looked up. "You sure you want to do this again?"

"Yes, I'm sure. I loved it. And I think I was good at it."

"All healed now? Strong again?"

"Yes."

"So come with me."

In the hallway he stopped a nurse going by and asked her to lie down on one of the stretchers along the wall. The nurse was surprised, but she lay down and adjusted her skirts. Then Matt Williams told Kate to pick up the stretcher at the back end and to raise it to shoulder height. He'd do the same at the front.

She remembered to change her grip halfway up, in a quick flip from overhand to underhand, and then to lock her elbows. It was tricky with a heavy load. During the flip you had to soften your knees for a moment.

"One more time," said Matt Williams. "Then hold her at a straight carry, and we'll walk to the door at the end and then we'll come back and put her down."

"All the way to the end?"

"Yes. Ready? At a good clip."

And they moved off. The nurse lay back, grinning up at her.

In the end the test went well, as did the second test, in which he asked her to drive him around several blocks in an ambulance truck at speed with the siren on.

"Not bad at all," he said back at the Emergency car park, after she'd set the handbrake. "Where'd you learn to drive like that?"

"During the Blitz, Mr. Williams."

"Really. Call me Matt. I liked that snappy downshift at the corner. Speeding up like that. Well done. In the Blitz, you say?"

"Yes."

"Good for you. So come with me, Kate. You're hired. I'll have them draw up formal papers, and I'll give you a uniform slip. You know what to do with it. Half shifts for the first month. And since it's been a while for you, you'll get extra training to upgrade your first aid. There are some new procedures and equipment for you to learn."

At the supply shed they gave her two complete uniforms: tunic, skirt, blouse, stockings, and cap. They also gave her a belt, two pairs of the brown shoes, and her kit bag.

She tried on the uniform and stood in front of the tall mirror.

"Fits all right?" said the woman behind the counter.

"Fits perfectly. I remember this."

"I was just going to say, I think I remember you. You were an ambulance girl before, weren't you?" The woman looked at the requisition slip. "Kate Henderson. What happened?"

In the afternoon she bicycled out to the horse farm. She had her jeans back on, and the boots and the Navy jacket. The air on her face was fresh and sweet, and birds sang on the wires and in trees.

When she turned the corner onto the farm driveway she couldn't resist ringing the bell, and immediately most of the horses in the paddocks raised their heads and some of them came trotting to the fence line. One of them . . . was it possible? One of them looked like Princess. A copper bay, the same white blaze down her face.

Mrs. Fitzhenry in her old wellies and a kerchief came out of the barn pushing a wheelbarrow full of hay. Looking tired. She set down the barrow and shielded her eyes.

"Kate! Is that you, girl?"

"It is, Mrs. Fitzhenry. And that horse . . ." She pointed. "Is that who I think it is?"

"It's Princess, yes. The new owners' business failed, and I bought her back. Even though I probably shouldn't have. Things are tight enough here as is."

Kate leaned her bicycle against the barn wall, grabbed a handful of hay from the wheelbarrow, and walked over to Princess. She rubbed her hands together to free the seeds. "Baby Horse," she said. "How are you? You were gone for a while too, weren't you? Here, have some of this. It's so nice to see you."

She looked over her shoulder at Mrs. Fitzhenry. "Can I ride her for a bit? Please?"

Mrs. Fitzhenry had picked up the wheelbarrow again. She looked at Kate and considered this. Then she said, "I heard you were in Canada. Is that right?"

"Yes, it is, Mrs. Fitzhenry. On a friend's horse farm in Nova Scotia. It was interesting. They had wild horses there and they were taming them."

"Were they now? Taming them for what?"

"Fresh blood for working horses. Like cow horses. They still have those over there. They still have cowboys, too."

"Cowboys!" said Mrs. Fitzhenry. "All right, you can exercise her. Not too hard. She hasn't been ridden in a while. Then you can groom her too."

"All right. How is Anne working out?"

"Fine. Fine. Go, girl. Do it."

The Seven Oaks path again, and up Shepherd's Hill and down into the valley. The ground good under the horse's unshod feet. Riding along, Princess and she were already in full agreement again, the horse nodding its head, walking the bridle path now among the springtime trees, everything lush and tender green, birch and oak and chestnut trees. A lush canopy and patches of wild ginger and deer fern on the ground. Once they were clear of the trees she moved Princess up into a trot and then for a short stretch across Ravens Field toward Fallen Rock into an easy canter with the breeze in her face and hair. So special all of this. So absolutely fine.

Back at the farm she led Princess to her stall, took off the saddle and put her into cross ties for grooming. Mrs. Fitzhenry came by and looked in.

"How did she do?"

"Fine, Mrs. Fitzhenry. She hasn't forgotten much. I think she's put on a bit of weight, has she?"

"She has. We weighed her."

"How long has she been back here with you?"

"A little more than a week. Ten days. Why?"

"I can get her into shape again, Mrs. Fitzhenry. Riding her, I was thinking . . . They hired me on again at Paramedics. So I have a good steady job and I also have some savings in the bank."

"Yes. What, Kate?"

"Are you still boarding other people's horses?"

"Yes, of course we are. It's an important part of our business."

"So I was thinking, Mrs. Fitzhenry. Could I buy Princess from you and stable her here? I would take full responsibility for her."

Mrs. Fitzhenry took a step back. "Kate . . . ," she said. She smiled and shook her head. "Look at you, Kate. Are you being serious?"

"Very much so, Mrs. Fitzhenry."

"Really?"

"Yes. Really."

"All right. So let's see. They paid one forty, her being a Morab and all, and I bought her back for one twenty. Can you afford that? Plus the stabling and feed on a monthly basis. And a vet bill now and then. It's not terribly much, and on days when you have time you could work some off by helping out. For riding her you could use our tack until you get your own."

"Yes, I can afford that, Mrs. Fitzhenry. Absolutely."

"All right. Then there's one more thing you need to know. Take a good look at her. See anything special?"

Kate took a step back and studied the horse. "She looks fine to me, and I didn't notice any injuries. Special in what way? Can you give me a hint?"

"I missed it too. But the vet didn't. He thinks she's pregnant. Early, but already more than fifty days past conception, which is why I could let you ride her. He can't do a urine test for another two weeks or so. Other than that, he says that Princess is healthy and all is well. So, tell me. Do you still want her?"

"Do I still want her?" Kate ran her hand down the horse's forehead. She rubbed the horse's cheek and said, "She's asking if I still want you, Baby Horse. Of course I do. I'll look after you. We'll do this together."

"Talk to me," said Mrs. Fitzhenry.

Kate turned around. "Do you have papers for the sire?"

"Not yet. They're sending them. I hear it's a good horse. So do you still want her? After full disclosure. Is it a deal?"

And with a big smile Kate said, "Yes, Mrs. Fitzhenry. Absolutely, it's a deal. One hundred and twenty pounds cash."

Mrs. Fitzhenry offered her hand, and Kate shook it.

Forty-seven

AT CLAIRE'S HOUSE, Delbert was on the telephone with Edward. Claire could hear him through the open kitchen door and could more or less guess the other side of the conversation.

Delbert was saying, "Finally. I've been leaving messages for you. And so has Kate. Greenwood, Winnipeg. Everywhere. And then someone gave me this number. Where are you?"

. . .

"I didn't know that. What do you mean you're this close? Oh, your wings. And then you're coming home?"

. . .

"I see. Kate told us about the Canadian citizenship thing. I hope you know what you're doing. Kate doesn't care if you're riding an airplane or a bicycle. She wants *you*."

. . .

"At some point, yes. A family. Children. That's what most women want sooner or later. If you want a woman, that's what you have to do. Men want to fly up and away, like you, but women are made differently."

. . .

"I know. I learned it too late. But about Kate, I want to help you avoid regrets. I love you, boy. Call her."

. . .

"Wait, I'll ask Claire."

Delbert leaned in by the door and said, "What's a good time for him to call Kate?"

"She's working now," said Claire. "And then she's got the first aid class. Have him call her today, later in the evening. After eight."

She listened to Delbert telling that to Edward. Then he said, "Kate's working at Paramedics again, and it looks like she'll also be putting in time at the physiotherapy place. They called her because they want her back. Things are changing here, Eddie, and Kate is making decisions. She's moving on, making a life for herself. She even bought a horse."

. . .

"She did. A week ago. A nice one. Claire and I saw it. Talk to her, Eddie. Be smart, okay?"

Claire heard him hang up the phone. He came into the kitchen and sat down. He looked at her and raised both hands off the table and put them down again. "I tried, didn't I? He said to say hello to you. I think he'll call her."

"I was listening in," she said. "You did your best."

She poured him tea, moved milk and sugar closer. She looked up at the clock. Time to go soon.

She watched him stir his tea and look at the steaming spoon before putting it down on the saucer. Ever since the day he told them his convent story, she'd liked this man. But then there had still been Patrick, and obligations to Thomas, in the background.

Delbert said, "My job with the city starts in two weeks and my days will be quite different then. It's a good job, Claire. Good pay. They confirmed it yesterday. And I think I found a flat, but I'm not sure I'm ready for it. I still like the Elgin place. Lost men, half of them, and I know and respect everyone's story there. We're like a family, Claire."

She smiled at him. There was that word again.

Forty-eight

TWO DAYS LATER, in the time between her paramedic shift and the first aid class, Kate sat typing another note to David. An update.

Looking back, there hadn't really been the need to burn her notes to him along with everything else. In a way they had been notes to herself as much as to him, but at the time she couldn't see that, or had forgotten it. All she could see were the men in long coats and hats and their magnifying glasses.

She rolled up the page to review what she'd written so far:

```
Dear David,

Eddie called me! I'm so happy. In a month he'll come

home for a week, on his way to Cairo. I love that boy,

and I know he loves me too. I think it was just that

he was so focused on getting his wings, and now he's

done it! Tomorrow there'll be a ceremony and all the

men left in his class will be presented with their
```

certificates. Apparently quite a few of them dropped
out. What's next, I'm not sure about. He'll be in Egypt
for a while, but I wouldn't want to pick up and leave
again. I have my job back at Paramedics, and at
physiotherapy Matron called me and she wants me too,
for twenty hours a week to begin with. I can do it for
now, and when Paramedics becomes full-time I'll see. So
I'm busy and I love it. Eddie and I, we'll work something out. We both really want to. That's my biggest
news, David. My happiest. The other good news is that
I bought a horse, and not just any old horse, but

What was that? . . . She looked up.

The front door had been opened and closed, and now she
could hear footsteps and low voices in the hallway behind her.
A man and a woman. Was that . . . was it Claire? Claire and who?

The footsteps came closer.

She listened for the man's voice. Stood up and raised a hand
to her heart, to her mouth.

The footsteps paused at her door. There was a gentle knock:
one . . . two, three.

And then she knew.

ACKNOWLEDGEMENTS

I wish to thank my editor, Kelly Joseph, for her many important contributions to *The Orphan Girl,* and I thank Jared Bland, my publisher, for his ongoing support. I also thank Sarah Howland, Sales Director; Adrienne Tang, Rights Director; Kimberlee Kemp, Managing Editor; Talia Abramson, Designer; Kim Kandravy, Production Coordinator; and Terra Page, Manager, Typesetting.

And a very big thank-you to you, Heather, always my first reader.

The Orphan Girl is Kurt Palka's eighth novel, following the best-sellers *The Piano Maker* and *The Hour of the Fox*. His previous book, *Clara* (*Patient Number 7* in hardcover), was shortlisted for the Hammett Prize. His work has been translated into eight languages. He lives near Toronto.